THIS BOOK

IS NOT

FOR YOU

THIS BOOK

IS NOT

FOR YOU

A NOVEL

DANIEL A. HOYT

DZANC
BOOKS

5220 Dexter Ann Arbor Rd.
Ann Arbor, MI 48103
www.dzancbooks.org

Library of Congress Cataloging-in-Publication Data

Names: Hoyt, Daniel A., author.
Title: This book is not for you / Daniel A. Hoyt.
Description: Ann Arbor, MI : Dzanc Books, [2017]
Identifiers: LCCN 2017003748 | ISBN 9781945814341
Classification: LCC PS3608.O9575 T48 2017 | DDC 813/.6--dc23
LC record available at https://lccn.loc.gov/2017003748

First US edition: November 2017
Interior design by Michelle Dotter

Printed in the United States of America

10   9   8   7   6   5   4   3   2   1

For Carolyn Doty, 1941-2003

CHAPTER ONE

I am born.

All right, that's out of the way.

This is not (not, not, not—pay attention to that word) a confession, a screed, a cry for help, a pack of lies, ghostly bullshit, or a murder mystery. It may be a rip-off of many other, better books—I'll give you that. That's a fair assessment. There's a murder in it, but I won't solve it. You won't solve it. We aren't going to unearth clues, dust anything (not to find fingerprints, not even to remove dust), interrogate anyone or some such shit. Don't look for clues. Don't come up with any "theories." Don't start thinking that I did it. Don't come up with any "interpretations." Don't get all Agatha Christie on me.

I know you will do these things anyway. I will be around the whole time to say, I told you so. Some fucked-up shit happened, which seemed awesome and mysterious at the time and perhaps should stay that way. I can't explain most of it, and it happened to me. My entire raison d'être is fucked-up shit, and all of this still makes no sense to me. Do you comprehend? I have never ever used the term raison d'être before, but I'm trying to speak your language. You have taken French, right?

You'll have to deal with some things. I will end sentences with prepositions. I will swear. I will fornicate. I will get intoxicated. I will annoy you.

I might become flippant about things you consider fragile and precious, and if I don't become flippant about things you consider fragile and precious, I'll probably wish I had.

This book is about Marilynne and skinheads and reading and drinking and Saskia and the black holes in our spirits. I use the term *spirits* metaphorically, just so we're clear, but this story is also about ghosts and time and the Ghost Machine and it might be about a bunch of other things, but it's not my job to figure that out.

That's where you come in.

Yes, you have rights, but you also have responsibilities.

In fact, here is a quiz you should take before you continue reading this book. Sharpen your pencil!

                                                    Yes   No

1. Do you dislike books that talk to you?
2. Do you want to solve mysteries?
3. Do you need an explanation for everything?
4. Do you dislike dirt, sex, profanity, and/or
     alcoholic beverages?
5. Do you suffer from night sweats, rapid heartbeat,
     and/or tinnitus?
6. Do you dislike quizzes?

That last question was a trick question. There are no more quizzes. Go back and take the quiz and pretend question six doesn't exist, and this time take the quiz like you fucking mean it.

I'll wait here.

OK, now give yourself one point for each yes.

* 5 points: Stop reading now and go wash your hands for a full thirty seconds. Burn this book in your backyard. Invite your friends—they probably have books they've been meaning to barbeque too. Also, apologize to your mother.

* 4 points: We don't want any.

* 3 points: Reply hazy, try again.

* 2 points: Proceed with caution.

* 1 point: It's only one point! That score practically doesn't exist.

* 0 points: Perhaps we are in love.

We are probably not in love. Love is a concept like Bigfoot. You need to want to believe. We are probably not in love, but I'm willing to at least acknowledge the possibility.

In all honesty, this is a grungy postmodern magical realist ghost story, with etiquette and grammar tips and all that shit. It's a picaresque. It's kind of a clap-trap noir.

I don't know why, but I almost forgot noir, your favorite French color.

It's also unadulterated pulp. It's pulpy as all get out. This is the straight juice, unstrained.

It might be a love story too, some kind of love.

Fuck if I know.

This is not a book for your mama's book group. Oprah is not here to guide you. There aren't any discussion questions in the back, like, "When Neptune and Saskia slam dance on page 151, it represents a surrender of hope to nihilism. What does your gentle and kindly soul think about this?"

We were just dancing. We like friction. There are no book group questions here, and if there were, you would not like the answers.

CHAPTER ONE

Which brings us back to that Wednesday. Maybe that Wednesday is when all of this really started. I wasn't a fetus. I was just about who I am now, minus a couple of months.

If you're one of those people who need to know what and when and in what proper order, I'm sorry. This must be pretty stressful to read.

Marilynne was alive then. I had known Marilynne for about two years. Sometimes she was a good kind of crazy.

She was calling on my cell phone. She was always calling on my cell phone. I sometimes shut it off. I sometimes left it at home. I sometimes said it was broken, even as she watched me talking on it.

If you have a phone, it will ring, buzz, chime, ding, play some song that sounded trampy even when it was a virgin, even the first time you heard it. Your phone will make demands. Your phone will connect you to other people, and it will make these connections staticky and unclear. You will not know where they are. You won't see the look on their faces. They might be on the toilet. They might be making the international symbol for "the human being on the other end of the line is a jerkoff." Your past will sometimes call you up. Sometimes it will text.

Your phone will let you take pictures. Your phone will let you access the Internet, which contains all of human knowledge and all of human disknowledge—which is not a word, but I discovered it via the Internet via my phone.

I tell you all this because my phone was blowing up. I wish it were literal, and, yes, there will be an explosion, but for now I am pedaling a metaphor.

I am not peddling. I'm not selling you anything.

I was known for stupid stuff. A fella can get a reputation like that. It's not hard.

Two separate factions wanted me.

One was Marilynne, a faction unto herself. The other was a group that specialized in stupid anarchist shit and they wanted to upgrade to bad shit. They wanted to get known real fast and in a big way. They wanted my help.

I was ignoring both of these factions.

I was where I almost always was, where bad ideas and hookups begin. I was at a bar, at the Replay to be exact, hanging out with a friend of mine, Uncle X, an old punk from Britain. He shows up a couple of times in this story, but he's not really part of it. He is but he isn't.

Uncle X draped his arm over my shoulder. He breathed in through his nose in a loud and jovial way. I felt the weight of his arm. Our bodies were scrunched together, and I could smell the Guinness from his glass, the Guinness on his breath. We were somewhere close to drunkenness.

The Replay has a couple of pinball machines, and a tiny stage for bands, and a long wooden bar. Through the glass front, you can stare out at Massachusetts Street. Outside, the back patio is about a hundred feet by fifty, surrounded by a seven-foot fence. It's all pressurized wood, some kind of deck stuff. The creatures of the night picnic out there, dance to old soul, laugh at things that aren't funny.

I can't remember what we were talking about, but I know I said, "What's next, Uncle X?"

"I don't know, mate," he said. "I don't know."

We watched a woman with smug breasts under a black turtleneck enter the Replay from the back patio. She waved to us.

"I think she's waving to me," Uncle X said.

"Us," I said.

"She has to be the smuggest woman I've seen in a while," he said.

"She even has smug feet."

"Smug arms!" Uncle X said, and then the woman was next to us, and Uncle X was pouring the thick black muck of beer into her glass.

"Neptune and I were just having a moment, love," Uncle X said. "Come on in. Come on in."

And then I think the three of us maybe hugged for a while, something like that.

Uncle X knew this smug woman somehow. She had been waving at him. I couldn't deny it anymore, and when my phone hissed in my pants to the left of my nuts, I broke from the scrummy hug. I went outside to answer.

I had missed all of these calls from Marilynne. Calvin, leader of the anarchists, had been calling me too.

It was him now. "Are you ready?"

"I told you I want no part of that shit," I said.

"Just come talk about it," Calvin said. "Come see the stuff."

You would think I would stop doing such asinine things, but I did want to see the stuff.

I figured it wouldn't hurt to look.

I peeked through the tinted window. Inside, Uncle X and the smug woman conspired over Guinness. Her smugness was distorted, smudged by the glass. If I had just stayed there and drank with them, this probably would have been a different book. This probably wouldn't have been a book at all.

I think this was my first bad narrative decision, but it's hard to keep track.

They're kind of my specialty.

CHAPTER ONE

All of this happened.

CHAPTER ONE

Life (n): the state in which stuff keeps happening.

Some of it was random, and some of it was planned out. Right before all of this began, a black mole in the shape of a comma appeared on my right thigh. I'm not joking. It was the pause between one thing and the next. Marilynne said she had one just like it. Perhaps her mole has surrendered into dust. Perhaps it was just one of Marilynne's stories. Perhaps I should have looked at it when I had the chance, but Marilynne is no longer engaged in this thing called life, which I have graciously defined for you.

My comma mole felt designed and shaped and destined for something. Last week, I cut it out with a Swiss Army knife. Now, I have this little comma scab.

Look closer. Here it is:

Go ahead and touch it if you want.

It didn't hurt that much. Yes, I sterilized the blade with a disposable lighter. It will heal. Flesh does that. And, by the way, I plan to leave the moles that look like periods as they are.

If you don't want to touch the scab, it's fine, and if you think I'm obnoxious and disgusting, well, I haven't really been obnoxious or disgusting yet. Not by my standards. I haven't even *tried* to be obnoxious or disgusting yet. I don't think I've tried to be much of anything yet. I haven't even introduced myself.

But first I have to tell you something, just in case you didn't know: A comma means something else is coming, more words. A comma means things ain't finished yet. I'd rather be a comma than an exclamation point, maybe even more than a question mark.

And, yes, I know that's not really a scab and I am not this book, but in some ways I am this book, and you know it.

Okay, sorry. Pleased to meet you and such. Where are my manners? My manners are reading a book. My manners are pedaling a mountain bike down by the Kaw. My manners are steaming at the bottom of a coffee cup.

I am not this book. I'm Neptune.

Five years ago, when the high school teacher with the overbite called the class roll, he said, "Let me know what you want to be called, you know, like a nickname or whatever," and we all stared blankly at him, and he stared back at us as if he had the knowledge to fill in the blanks, and he read his carefully ordered names. We were all lined up alphabetically. He read them with a deep, loud voice, and then smaller, shallower voices said "Here" and sometimes "Yo."

I don't remember what class it was. When he read my name, I just blurted out, "Neptune." I thought people would laugh, but no one did.

The teacher said, "Neptune?"

And I said, "Neptune," and then he wrote the name down on his roll sheet, and he said quietly and thoughtfully, "Neptune," and ever since, I've been Neptune. His overbite made it seem serious. I had nothing else to make me seem serious. I was on something called "academic probation" and something else called "home release" and something else called "Quaaludes." All of those things wore off after a while. And that's about all that I got out of high school: a name.

I can't even think of myself in any other way. I *am* Neptune.

Neptune is the blue planet. I've read that winds there blow at seven hundred miles per hour, but I'm not sure how we know this. This smells like a guesstimate to me.

I'm Neptune, and I'm full of poisons, and I come fully endorsed by the teacher with the overbite, whatever his name was, whatever his class was.

I've been shaving since twelve. I've been six foot one since fourteen. I've lived on my own—on the streets, off the streets—since fifteen. I've lived for eons, and I just turned nineteen.

I have a really good fake ID. I've had to fake some things forever.

You'd think I was older. Maybe you thought that already.

I have a small scar, about a quarter-inch long, to the left of my left eye, and if anyone asks about it, I look at them in a square, fierce way and say, "Knife fight," and then I laugh. But the truth is it did happen in a knife fight.

For a while I hung out with the skinheads, but my hair is back now, and I don't see ghosts at all anymore. They're not that kind of skinheads anyway.

I got my GED when I was seventeen. I got these scholarships to study English at the University of Kansas and a Pell grant, and I might have been a genius if I wasn't so stupid. I had been homeless for a while. I had been in juvenile detention. That's not all of it.

Marilynne was an English professor when I first met her, about two years before she ended up dead, and then I don't know what she was. A ghost, I guess. Maybe some other language has a better word, but it's all I've got.

There's other stuff I should tell you, but I don't feel like getting into all of that right now.

Isn't that enough to start? How far do you have to go back to find the beginning? I don't plan on becoming a fetus for you.

Haven't I told you about my name? Haven't I shown you my scab? I let you touch it! Isn't that enough for now?

CHAPTER ONE

You hate me already. I can tell.

CHAPTER ONE

The anarchists lived about six blocks away. I walked there on the kind of early night that has some sort of possibility to it, maybe clouds, maybe stars, maybe lightning on the way to stars.

This is Kansas: *Ad Astra Per Aspera*, which means *To the stars through difficulties*. That's the state slogan, thought up by the abolitionists in search of a slave-free state in the 1800s. I've got it tattooed on my hip. I did it myself with guitar string. I medicated with beer, traced those letters with careful pain, and bled into an old T-shirt. It's my best tattoo. Yes, I spelled everything right.

With the exception of seventeen and a half days, when I hitchhiked to San Francisco and back a summer ago, I've breathed every one of my breaths in Kansas or Missouri, those two states that hated each other around the Civil War, but you know that—or you should. Look it up. I'm generally found in Kansas, the Free State, and, yes, there's a bar here in Lawrence called the Free State too, but I only go there on Mondays when pints are half price. I'm talking about the greater metaphysical, geographical region of freedom, and, yes, I use the term *metaphysical* without having a true sense of its definition, but I feel it, you know? If you don't feel words, maybe we need to call quits on this whole literary partnership, this whole fucking expedition.

Fucking is a word I feel too. It's a striated muscle. Anyway, Google *metaphysical*. Google *Bloody Kansas*. I'm not going to give you a history lesson. I've got other things to write. This book is on the way to see the anarchists. Those assholes had their own plans for blood.

I just wanted to see the stuff.

Those assholes rented a large green Victorian on Kentucky Street.

In Lawrence, the main east-west streets were named for the United States as they entered the Union, each in their proper order—state No. 1 Delaware to the south, then No. 2 Pennsylvania, No. 3 New Jersey, and so on, with No. 6 Massachusetts Street cutting the main downtown swath because the abolitionists came from Massachusetts.

The abolitionists came first, and the bars along Mass came later. The bars are named with less precision than the streets. The Replay Lounge, Harbour Lights, the Taproom, the Red Lyon.

I don't think the abolitionists would have imagined me or the bars or the anarchists, although maybe they'd understand everything all too well. A Confederate guerrilla named William Quantrill marched in and burned this town in 1863. His raiders killed men, boys too: 183 in all.

And here I am, giving a history lesson.

CHAPTER ONE

I walked fast. I always walk fast. That's because you're always fleeing destruction, Saskia says.

The house looked too nice, too neat, too landscaped to shelter anarchists.

I didn't knock. That was one of the things anarchists didn't believe in.

Two dudes I didn't know were playing Xbox in the living room. They weren't townies.

"Who the fuck are you?" one of them asked.

"Neptune."

"Fucking A," he said. "Get Calvin."

"You get Calvin."

"It's my turn," the first guy said, mashing his controller.

The other guy went to get Calvin.

I could describe these guys to you, but it wouldn't matter. It only matters to their mothers and their girlfriends, their boyfriends, their mirrors, occasionally an eyewitness, often the cops. Mainly can I say that I don't remember? Will you use that against me later when I say things you don't believe and you want to accuse me of fictionalizing all the weird shit that happened? I forgot what those losers looked like, but I didn't forget the important stuff.

"Neptune," Calvin said. He reached down to shake my hand. Calvin had hands the size of roast beefs. He was humongous, six foot seven or something. He's one of the only people I know who's a lot bigger than me. If you look at video clips of the World Trade Organization riots in Seattle on YouTube, look for the huge anarchist in the black ski mask. That's him. Calvin outgrew anonymity in eighth grade. He was bald but not a skinhead. Instead of your hand, he shook your whole arm up to the pit.

"I'm just here to see the stuff," I said.

He didn't let go of my arm, but he stopped levering it like a pump handle.

"Guys," Calvin said, "this is our special guest."

"Shit," one of the video game players said, and they both got up, and they left the game on. Its digital forces kept trying to destroy them anyway.

"You want a beer?" Calvin said. There's only one answer to this question: I always want a beer. In the kitchen, we found two young women and some beer, plus a couple of other dudes playing quarters.

"This is our special guest," Calvin said. "This is Neptune." Calvin and the two video game players stood really close to me.

I was starting to mistrust the word *special* and the word *guest*. I drank my beer anyway.

"Let's go take a look," Calvin said.

He led me down a hallway, and a woman in a Pantera shirt followed us.

"Not now, sweetie," Calvin said. She shrugged at us, and Calvin said to me, "Come on."

He led me into a room where a black backpack sat on a bare double bed.

"Take a peek," he said.

I unzipped the bag and looked at the dynamite: six sticks, each as fat as a baseball bat, about a foot long. The white string fuses were braided together: light one fuse, and they'd all blow.

"I expected it to feel eviler," I said.

"It's enough to destroy the whole building," Calvin said. Then he paused, cleared his throat, said, "You in?"

I hadn't done anything violently stupid or stupidly violent for a couple of years, but once you're dirty like that, you never get clean.

All the worst shit I did happened when I was thirteen, fourteen. All that shit's supposed to be sealed. I'm supposed to be innocent again.

Well, not exactly innocent. Free to start anew.

But when you have a reputation for stupid stuff, it follows you around. A guy in Wichita once offered me nine hundred bucks to run his ex-wife off the road. The cops used to question me once a month: *Do you know anything about that knifing outside the frat-boy bar?*

Calvin wanted me to walk up to the University of Kansas campus, use Marilynne's keys to unlock Wescoe Hall in the middle of the night, plant dynamite, set an electronic timer, and get the hell out of there. Calvin had talked about this plan for a year. He had never actually had dynamite before. I had thought he was bullshitting. He had talked about blowing up other things: the campanile, Allen Fieldhouse, the AT&T tower behind the Eldridge Hotel, the transformer station east of downtown. He deemed some of these things too beautiful, and some would cause collateral damage.

A few months earlier, over a bottle of vodka, Calvin insisted he didn't want to kill anyone. He wanted to wake people up.

"To what?" I asked.

"All of our experiences are fake," he said, and then he changed the channel on the TV. "I'm aware of the irony," he said, nodding at the TV. "I need to be woken up too."

You'd think I would have stopped associating with people like that, but I wasn't really associating. I was just breathing the same air, drinking the same liquor.

Now Calvin actually had the dynamite. He was fucking serious.

"No one will be there, dude," he said. "We've been watching every night. No one's in there from, like, two to six. Nobody's dying, I promise."

"No way," I said.

"We'll do it now, tonight. No one'll miss that building—big old punk-ass garage-like piece of shit."

I didn't say anything.

"We'll slip in, set a timer, sneak out."

"I don't want any part of this shit, Calvin."

"No one will know, dude," he said. "Wescoe is the only building on campus without security cameras. No one cares if it gets trashed."

He looked at me with all of his bulk, one eyebrow cocked up, one hand working in and out of a fist. I'd fought guys almost as big before. I tried not to make a habit of it.

"I don't have the keys," I said.

"We'll go get them from the old lady, me and you."

He meant Marilynne.

"I don't think so, Cal."

"I thought you believed in anarchy! I thought you believed in not giving a shit!"

I had always believed in not giving a shit—it's my birthright—but not like that.

He was breathing hot death down at me. He was holding onto my arm.

"We've got to send a message to this state, this governor, this country." Every time he said *this*, he squeezed a bruise into my biceps. "This is an act of civil disobedience!"

He pulled me back down the hallway and planted another beer in my hands. He sort of nodded at the woman in the Pantera shirt.

"We need you," Calvin said.

"We need his fucking keys! We don't need him," one of the guys playing quarters said.

"That's true," Calvin said. "We could just beat the shit out of you, Neptune. Or worse."

"Let me think about it," I said. "Let me get a cigarette."

"Who's the skinny?" the woman asked.

"Neptune," Calvin said. "He used to be known as a solid guy." Then he looked at me, tipped his pack of Marlboros in my direction, said, "Think!"

"Think hard!" somebody else said.

Maybe you're already aware that thinking isn't one of my specialties.

Calvin went to the front room to watch TV. He tuned into something brutal on the History Channel. I could tell from the solemn narrator, the sound of explosions.

I smoked with one hand, and with the other I held the cold can of beer up to my forehead as a catalyst. Still no thoughts. I began to administer it orally.

"You want to play quarters?" a wiry guy asked. He had a snaggletooth.

I shook my head.

The woman in the Pantera T-shirt now pressed up against me.

"He knows what we need him to play," she said.

One of her breasts rubbed on my arm. Her eyes were kind but blasted out. She probably hooked up with Calvin most of the time.

"Let me think a bit," I said.

"About what?" she said, and her breast whooshed across my arm again.

If I had lived like a monk, I'd be a goner. I was never a monk. I was always a goner, though. I was a born goner.

"Let me think on it," I said.

She kissed me on the forehead, right above the left eye— a slimy blessing—then wandered off. I could hear a heavy bass beat in one room and the television in the other. The quarters players were fucked up beyond coordination.

I flitted like a moth to the sources of light: the TV, the refrigerator, the room with the dynamite, back to the TV.

At the anarchists' house, none of the clocks had the right time. None of the clocks had the same time. Time became malleable.

Time became a guess.

"Will you chill out?" Calvin said.

"I'm too alive," I said.

CHAPTER ONE

Neptune is the god of the sea, but everybody likes Poseidon better.

Everybody likes Aquaman better.

It's the blue planet because of all the methane in the atmosphere. I don't usually broadcast this.

I'm Neptune, and I like long walks on the beach.

I was trying not to do shitty things. I was trying not to do the things I did.

I don't like cookouts.

I like to turn those pages fast.

CHAPTER ONE

I wandered again to the room with the dynamite. The backpack just sat on the bare mattress—it had a big round stain, and someone had written "Sergio did this" with a magic marker in the middle of the stain. The backpack wasn't that heavy really. I slipped the straps over my shoulders. You'd think something so deadly would have some real weight, but it just felt full of paperbacks. There's no harm in those, except to your thoughts, except to your soul.

I adjusted the straps, and it felt snug, right somehow. I walked out into the hallway and then down the hall to an old sun porch. A man and a woman were making out on a futon, hands down each other's Dickies, up each other's T-shirts.

"I'll be right back," I said, then I clicked out the back door. I closed the door really carefully.

I walked a couple of steps into the backyard. It was unfenced, unmowed, unlit. I took some even, casual strides. I waved and puffed my cigarette, like I was taking the air, saving them all from my pollutants. It was a strange foggy night all of a sudden, and the air felt slick. I circled the yard, then took a wide turn out into the back alley parallel to Ohio.

Then I ran like a motherfucker.

When I was about halfway down the block, I heard a crash—a door being thrown open. Then Calvin yelled "Neptune!" in a B-movie type of way, and I always thought I was stupid and histrionic, but maybe everyone is stupid and histrionic. I didn't think they could see me from the house, but I ran harder anyway. If I had to, I thought maybe I could do it: blow myself up. I had my lighter in my pocket, right next to my phone, which was vibrating away. Those Buddhist monks do it slow, but I wouldn't.

I realize that this, too, is stupid and histrionic, but I really thought about it, becoming a big human fireball and then, for eternity, being nothing. At that point, I didn't believe in ghosts. Do you see how I know nothing, and how on each page I grow dumber? Be careful—as Dr. Cobain said, stupidity's contagious.

I knew who was calling. I looked anyway: Calvin. He could make my pants vibrate, but I didn't have to pick up.

I sprinted down the alley for a couple of blocks, and then I turned, heading down Tenth toward downtown. I was still booking it. My lungs were sacks of crumpled paper. My heart was a reactor. It felt like a meltdown. I had an explosion on my back. I had an explosion in my chest.

I have no idea if stealing the dynamite was incredibly smart or incredibly stupid. So many of my decisions live in that deadland.

Out on the street, the beautiful people who wanted to be scuzzy were trying to differentiate themselves from the scuzzy people who wanted to be beautiful. It's not as easy as you might think. I had my own scuzzy veins and lungs and skin.

My lungs said, "And yes and yes and yes and yes." My heart said, "And yes and yes and yes and yes."

I followed these affirmations all the fuck back to the Replay.

CHAPTER ONE

If you don't like profanity, then fuck you.

CHAPTER ONE

I suppose I had better tell you about Marilynne.

Two years ago, I had a work-study job where I made photocopies of photocopies for professors in the English Department at the University of Kansas, which for a very short time considered me a student in good standing and then a student in not-so-good standing and then someone who wasn't welcome on campus.

On the day I met her, I had a big pile of fresh smudgy words, and I knocked on her barren office door. Other professors taped up postcards in French and souvenirs of horrible academic excursions (Popular Culture Studies in South Dakota!). Marilynne had a brass nameplate that said "M. Hobson."

I didn't know what the M. signified. I knocked, and I could hear breathing on the other side, but the door didn't open. I knocked again and the breathing rattled on. I knocked some more.

"Who is it?" someone asked.

"Neptune," I said.

"We don't want any," she said.

"Copies," I said, and the door opened.

"There's the young scribe," she said.

Her voice had a tease in it, but it wasn't unkind. She seemed about sixty, and her hair was the gray of dishwater. She sat me down in the office. She made me chicken bouillon with a mug of hot tap water. It tasted like watery salt. She listed three other professors whom she hated to various degrees. That's roughly what I remember. I was supposed to be making more copies.

"I feel like I'm looking in a mirror," she said to me. I looked right back at her, at her plump pink face and her gray hair.

I didn't say anything, which was the clever strategy I had worked out for dealing with any and all authority figures.

She said, "You have your mirrors, I have mine."

She was always getting copies made. I was always making them.

She was cracking up. I knew it, and I even drove her to a doctor's office once, and she sat in the car in the parking lot, and she wouldn't get out, and she called me a cunt fucker, which is not inaccurate but seemed unrelated to her mental well-being.

Besides the skins, whom I didn't even hang with anymore, she was maybe the closest I had to family.

I made her bed and did her laundry. I brought her meals from the Mad Greek. I sometimes read books to her.

When I started taking classes, when I started working for the English Department, she's the one who said I belonged.

Maybe you can blame her for all of this.

Not for what happened.

For the fact that you have to read about it.

CHAPTER ONE

Did you notice I used whom right in that last chapter? Or maybe I didn't. I might have rewritten that part.

I might not even know the right rules.

But don't think that I'm lying to you. I won't lie to you—because I love you as much as I can love a complete stranger. And you can love a complete stranger. Try it some night, some afternoon, at a laundromat, in an airport, at a library. We're already twenty-eight pages in, and I haven't lied to you yet. Go back and review. Do your due diligence.

And I promise that I'm not going to say, "I'm not going to lie," and then lie anyway. That's not what this is all about. It's not really about alcohol or Marilynne or commas or Lawrence or sadness or ghosts or murder or the Ghost Machine or skinheads or dynamite, so maybe I lied about all of that. It's about sitting down and reading a book. Let's just say that's what it's about. Go ahead. Keep going.

It's not really my fault if you can never find your place in this thing. That's on you.

Get a fucking bookmark or something.

And if you're bored, you can skip Chapter One.

CHAPTER ONE

I wasn't kidding when I said I needed to think. I still hadn't thought, hadn't thunk.

I couldn't go home, and the anarchists would probably check in on some of my friends.

I ran some more, backpack heavy as a motherfucker, then I jogged, then I walked.

I had to get somewhere that would take me in.

I'd be safest at the bars. The anarchists could find me, but they wouldn't be able to do shit with all of the people around. That was my theory anyway, but remember this wasn't exactly thinking—this was feeling. This was spiritual.

I had my breath back. I was headed to the Replay. It almost seemed like a normal night again, and when Marilynne called—each of her calls delivered a distinct snake-like buzz—I answered it.

"Yes," I said, and it wasn't even a nice yes. It was flat and hard, a two-by-four of affirmation. You swing that kind of yes at someone.

"Can you come over here? Can you come over here, please?" Marilynne said.

I chewed on my lip. I made a clicking sound with my tongue. I adjusted the backpack full of dynamite that I had just stolen. I stretched out time. I was standing on Massachusetts Street again, outside the Replay, and I could hear the muffled thrum of music leaking out of the windows. I knew I shouldn't go home, that various anarchists would be headed that way. Marilynne was breathing on the other end of the line. It sounded like aerosol spritzing from a can.

"Are you okay?" I asked.

"No," she said, "not really."

"Oh, Christ," I said, and then I said it again.

"Will you stop saying 'Oh, Christ'?"

"Oh, Christ," I said, and then I listened to more of her spray-can gasps.

"I'm coming to see you," I said. "Give me a few minutes."

I knocked on a tinted window at the Replay, but no one seemed to notice or care. If I had been on the other side of that glass, I wouldn't have given a shit either. I could see a gray splash of myself reflected in the window, and inside I could see the shapes of pinball machines and a few regulars and Missy behind the bar. I could see that fucking asshole Tax with his stupid cymbal hands.

The night sent a cold swirl of wind slinking down the back of my neck, and I zipped up my hoodie. I shrugged my backpack up and down.

It started to become clear to me that I had done something stupid. Sure, it was an attempt to stop people from doing something even stupider, something deadly even, terroristic. But outside of the Replay, I felt drunk with dumbness.

I watched Tax clap his hands together so that the stupid fucking brass rings he wore chimed. He did it all the time, but I couldn't hear it on this side of the glass. I could see everything going on but couldn't hear his metallic shitbag noise; I could only hear the throb of the jukebox. Out here the song was muffled enough so I could just barely not recognize it. It felt like part of my subconscious, and I almost went in to find out what that aspect of me really sounded like. What were the lyrics? I knocked again, and nobody flinched on the other side of the glass. When I felt pessimistic, life was a knock-knock joke where no one says, "Who's there?" When I felt optimistic, life was a knock-knock joke where you have to listen to the punch line.

No one at the Replay wanted to who's-there me.

Only Marilynne wanted to who's-there me. It made me feel like a crumpled-up aluminum can.

I pumped my crumpled aluminum can legs and crumpled aluminum can arms, heading down Mass. I was turning onto Eleventh. I was turning onto New Hampshire. I was heading down New Hampshire. I had a crumpled tin can nose. I'd never get all of those wrinkles out of me. Once the can's squished, smooth is a memory.

My head felt sodden with beer. At that point in my life, I had never read *Huck Finn*. It seems important now, but, then, I had some kind of hole in me where *Huck Finn* was supposed to go. I didn't think about *Huck Finn* on that walk, or Saskia or the skins or the dynamite or even Marilynne really. I didn't even think about the Ghost Machine or sex or whiskey or Casey. I bet you're jealous, but I used to be able to think about nothing at all, to create a vast, pure fermata of the brain. I could just be.

I walked by all the nice wooden houses of all the nice wooden people. The people aren't all wooden, actually. That's not fair. Some of them are actually brick.

The night hung over everything. It dripped off the streetlamps. My phone bleated again. Calvin had called me six times and left five messages. But this time, it was Marilynne again.

"I'm coming," I said into the little piece of plastic and zinc or whatever the fuck, and two blocks away the words zapped into her ear.

Outside her house, I looked at the shrubs, and I said the word "shrubbish" out loud because I liked the librarian shh-shh of it. An off-white fence ringed the yard, and a brick walk led up to a mauve door. The house itself was a bitter green; it looked like mouthwash. I creaked open the gate, and I took a deep breath, and I sprinted up the walk. The gate slammed shut behind me. I ran right up to the door and turned the knob and pushed with a shoulder and flew in.

When you entered Marilynne's house, it felt like you had become possessed by mauve. It striped her walls. It assaulted her couches and her pillows. She kept the windows sealed up, and the air seemed trapped in there with the colors—the mauve, the accents of crimson, of sea foam. During one of those months when she refused to go outside, she talked constantly of redecorating. She acquired swatches of fabric and little cards of fancy paint colors—"Egyptian Hummus," that kind of shit—that she would stick on the wall and squint at. She'd stare as if she could turn two inches of color into an entire wall. She liked to tell me about those colors. She showed me scraps of fabric.

"Touch it," she would say, and I would run my fingers over the velvet.

"It feels like mauve," I would say.

She liked to talk about getting the whole house redecorated, but the only thing that changed was a fresh coating of dust, bits of her skin that she sucked up with a vacuum cleaner. You had to fight with that vacuum cleaner, wrestle and shake it, and steal the bag of guts from it. I emptied it for her. Sometimes it felt like

I was dumping out the equivalent of a body part: a foot of dust, two and a half ears' worth.

The constant, empty wish to redecorate came after the parties—years and years of parties—but before her complete fear of people. She gave big, floppy parties, and people would drink and talk about books until the night drained away and their bones turned to drippy wax. They would wake up in corners and on couches, search for the puddles of their brains. I had rematerialized there before, too many times. Most of the people who came to the parties didn't come around much anymore. They weren't welcome anyway.

She still had the liquor, sure. But the thump of music, of thought, of fun that turns to its opposite in the morning, was gone. Only the opposite was there now, and it hung around all day, fogging up the rooms.

I might have thought about all these things then; I don't remember really. But I think about them now. That night when I smashed through her door and into her mauveness, her mauvosity, she sat calmly on the couch. She held a TV remote in her left hand. Her right hand glittered with shards of glass and a wet sheen of blood. I could see clear spikes poking out of her fingers and her palm. Marilynne didn't seem to notice at all.

"Do you want to see my comma mole?" she asked.

She was sixty-two years old, and she had a moon-shaped face, pale blue eyes that bulged a bit more than normal out of their sockets; they were trying to climb out at you. She was just under five feet tall, and she liked to call herself "a little person." She was only being partly ironic. She always liked being partly something: partly annoying, partly funny. On that night, she was wearing a flowered dress that looked vaguely Hawaiian. It bordered the territory between silk and polyester. It was big and shapeless, like most of the things she wore. Sometimes I thought Marilynne wanted to forget that she owned a body.

If we were exact and responsible investigators, I wouldn't try to summon up her face; I'd tell you the exact times of things. We'd calibrate and syncopate and recreate the entire evening, but all I can tell you is it was Wednesday night, unless it was that part of Thursday morning that we still consider Wednesday night. I can tell you that her nose was a girlish and gentle bump; a bit of her moon face slouched past her chin; she had false teeth that were too white and too straight to ever seem real. She wanted them to seem real. She wanted her nose to be bigger now to catch up with her protruding eyes. She wanted her gray hair to fade back to blonde. She had told me all these things, and I remember them. But I'm totally fucked if I have to tell you the time.

CHAPTER ONE

It happened at some point in time.

"What the fuck did you do?" I asked.

Marilynne rubbed her right thumb across her right fingers several times, the way people do when they mean money, but she didn't mean anything at all. She clicked the remote, and the muted TV shifted to another wordless spasm of color.

"It's just stuck," she said, "stuck, stuck."

She rubbed her hand against her face, and a rusty crimson smear appeared on her forehead.

"You're fucking bleeding," I said, because that's the kind of astute and perceptive person I am. The blood sprouted from her forehead now too. I could see it bubbling up, and I grabbed her hand, looked at it. It sparkled with shards of glass.

"What the fuck, Marilynne? What the fuck?"

It was a question I had asked her before.

I picked each shard out with tweezers, collected them in a cereal bowl. We just sat there on the couch, and she didn't flinch, didn't cry, didn't say much, probably didn't feel. I counted: eight of them. How did it happen?

She didn't know. She didn't know. She didn't know.

"Maybe a glass broke in my hand," she said.

As I pulled them out, I pictured her stabbing each one of them in, getting to eight before she called me on the phone. She probably thought about nine. She probably liked the idea of it, but she probably liked the evenness of eight. I didn't ask. Accidents don't look like that. Accidents look like a scrawl, a squiggle. This was penmanship.

"You did this on purpose," I said.

She looked at me with her bland moon-pie face. On the television, a bigger face, larger than larger than life, made shapes with his lips that probably formed words.

We listened to the last shard plink into the cereal bowl.

I wiped my hands on my jeans and poured myself a drink. Whiskey straight. I poured an inch on top of another inch.

"Should I call 911?" I asked.

She was pulling herself together. I could see something liquid wash back into her eyes. She got up out of the living room, and I swirled whiskey around my mouth, tasting mauve. The big face on the TV seemed to be shouting. Marilynne had taken the remote, so I got up and punched the man right in the off button. He died on the spot.

I could hear the rush of water from the bathroom down the hall.

"Clean that shit out good," I yelled.

She came back with a roll of gauze and a plaid oven mitt.

"Do the honors?" she asked, and I wrapped up those fingers of hers, her still bloody palm.

"You'll live," I said.

She pulled the oven mitt over the gauze.

"That's a good look for you," I said.

I've broken glasses in my hand, gripped and gripped until the pressure was too great. It makes an awful steely pop, and shards snap out, and I've cut a few fingers, gashed a palm. It doesn't leave shards in your hand. That takes an entirely different kind of pressure.

"What was that all about?" I asked.

"I needed to get you over here," she said.

"But you didn't say anything on the phone."

"You knew. You could hear it in my voice."

How could I say that I didn't hear anything at all? I almost didn't answer the phone. If someone had looked up at the Replay, I would have gone right inside. I had thought about hanging up on her. I had thought about saying, "Fuck off. Not tonight. No way." The pain I had heard was everyday pain. We all carry that caliber of hurt in our back pocket.

"You got lucky," I said.

We sat on the couch and watched the big dark TV. It was the safest place to look. I could hear the soft thwap of Marilynne tapping her oven mitt again her leg.

"I'm giving you this house," she said.

I just sort of laughed. When I looked at her, though, her mouth was a flat line of sneer.

"I'm not so good at owning stuff," I said.

She had given me stuff before: a taxidermied bat, a six-gallon tin of caramel corn, a couple thousand dollars, several copies of the books she had written. I had thrown the stuffed bat off a roof at a house party as sort of a joke. I lost the popcorn tin at the Replay. I lost the money at every bar in town. I sold the books at the Dusty Bookshelf. She had probably seen those books for sale in there, reread the inscriptions, died a little bit. I only remember one of them:

Dear Neptune,
I can't say enough about any of this.
With all my love,
Marilynne

In all that time, I had never read one of her books.

~~I didn't want to risk it. What if I loved them? What if I hated~~ them? What if I felt nothing?

She would know that I had read them. She could read the bumps on my face, my hair follicles, my smells. My body would sweat out criticism, and her nose would pull it in, and she would never forgive me, not even if I thought she was a genius. I knew her too well already. She knew me too well already. We needed boundaries.

She could call me up and mumble in my ear; I took out her garbage; I pointed out that strangers loitering outside her window were most likely benign. I didn't need to spend time in another world she'd created. I already lived in one.

"Fuck you," she said. She was back to being her. Her face shriveled up into an angry raisin. She pushed herself up off the couch and marched out of the room. She took big showy footsteps so I could hear each one as she pounded down the hallway, yanked open a door, then smashed down the basement steps. I thought about following, but then my cellphone neighed at me.

"Hello," I said.

"Hey," Casey said, "where are you?"

"Marilynne's."

"Wanna hang out?"

"Of course," I said.

"Meet me at the Replay for last call."

"I was just there," I said.

"Come on."

"I'm coming," I said and clicked off.

"Coming where?" Marilynne said. She had a can of spray paint in her oven-mitt claw.

"The Replay. My work here is done."

"Fuck you," Marilynne said. She shook up the can of spray paint. The balls pinged around inside. She snapped the plastic cap off the can, and it flew across the room. Then she got to work. Right across the mauve, she painted a big black vertical line and then a diagonal one and then another vertical:

N

I just watched, drank up the last of the whiskey. She had given up teaching. I brought her groceries. I drove her car around corners. When the cable dude came, I answered the door while she hid in the basement. Since I had known her, she had been falling apart, sometimes willfully, and now there wasn't much binding her together. She needed more things than she could imagine. She usually just said she needed gin, sometimes tonic. She needed a lot more than I could supply.

She kept going. She seemed to breathe in concert with the can. They made horrible gaseous hisses together. She inflicted those big black letters, and, of course, by the time she got to the first e or the p, I knew the whole story. She did it the way I do it sometimes, with the big N's and little everything elses.

Her vertical strokes were shaky, and her horizontal strokes were even worse, and her breath huffed with the paint.

"With those big N's it almost looks balanced," she said. "Right? Isn't that the point?"

I talked to my whiskey in a silent language. The paint kept pulsating out onto the wall. By the time her breath and the paint ran out, it said this:

NeptuNe's HouSe

"I don't want a house," I said.

"Doesn't matter. It's yours now," she said. "I'm giving it to you. I just gave it to you. Your name's on it."

"I don't want a house," I said, and I grabbed my bag of dynamite, and I checked my phone. Calvin had left three more messages.

"I don't want a house," I said again.

That's the last thing I said to her as I walked out the door.

CHAPTER ONE

In the early twenty-first century, a gentlewoman or gentleman might receive a phone call for the purpose of arranging sexual intercourse. These timely summonses usually, but not always, occurred in the nighttime. Colloquially speaking, they were known as "booty calls."

Sometimes, of course, people received calls for entirely different reasons.

CHAPTER ONE

There's sex on pages 53, 55, 153, 171, 175. There's fucked-up titillation on page 121. There's a splash of lust on page 255. You already know there's a breast on page 21.

CHAPTER ONE

Property of Neptune.

CHAPTER ONE

Deep inside my chest, a long false fingernail scratched at my lungs, chipped my ribs. It wanted to tear away my aorta. I know I swallowed it somehow. It formed from smoke and carcinogens, stolen dynamite, microwaved plastic, whiskey and hurt feelings. I had asked for it. The point of it was cruelty. The point of it pried up and under my sternum. I felt like I could move it around under my skin. I felt like I could never sleep it off. Sometimes the nails from the rest of the fingers were up in my brain. Sometimes I could feel the color change: black, hydrant red, mauve, mauver.

Marilynne never wore fingernails like that. In fact, I can't remember her fingernails at all. She must have had them. Aren't they, like, a package deal with fingers?

I don't know anyone with fingernails like that, but, still, I wake up with them stuck in me.

I could feel one scratching away as I left the house, but I clipped it right out of my mind. As I swept down the street, I left all ideas of Marilynne back at the house, *her* house. She would call me up in two days to paint over my name. We'd cover it all up.

I could smell sex and cold in the air, and I flipped up my hoodie again. Outside it was a normal night, and back at Marilynne's it had kind of been a normal night too. I looked up for stars and found the wool of clouds. I breathed in and let oxygen settle in my lungs. I walked fast. I was just about to turn off of New Hampshire when I saw him coming toward me, first just a black shape, then a man, then motherfucking Tax.

There's only one chance to make that first miserable, lasting impression, they say, but that's bullshit. I'm newly unimpressed with people all the time.

He had a little pointed beard but no mustache. His hair was black, and his blue eyes were soft and wounded. You could tell that he knew girls liked this about them. You could see him softening them sometimes. He probably practiced. He blinked a lot. He drank PBR at the Replay. He seemed to have no other particular places to go. He had those fucking cymbal hands: he wore a ring on every finger, and when he cracked his hands together they made a sound that might have been melodic or might have been noise. He clapped his hands all the time. He had one of those chains for a wallet, but he didn't carry a wallet. He just stuffed his bills in a pocket. His voice sounded scratched and burnt, like he had just swallowed a cigarette. He was a couple inches taller than me. We knew each other in the way that two people who don't like each other know each other.

"Hey," I'd say, and he'd pause and say "Hey" back. He'd pause just long enough for me to remember what an asshole he was and would always be.

That's all I knew about him. Also, he dealt drugs in Topeka. We slept with a couple of the same women. He had a name that I always pretended to forget.

Could he kill a person? It was pretty obvious he could do anything that assholes do.

Could I kill a person? Likewise.

Why would anyone kill her? She didn't have anything worth taking. She didn't hurt anyone, not really.

Earlier that night, when I looked through the glass, I had seen him clap his hands together to make the metallic clash, but I couldn't hear it. It was a soundless sound. It seemed to mean something. And now, here he was.

"Where the fuck are you going?" I asked.

He paused the asshole pause.

"To conduct business," he said. "You?"

"To fuck into a reverie."

"Yeah right," he said.

I got my face right up into his. His baby-soft eyes hardened up. If I stuck out my tongue, I would have licked his cheek. We stood that way. His eyes flipped from hard to soft to nothing. He stepped back.

"I don't have time for this shit," he said.

"Pussy," I said. I felt the hot happy blood of violence pumping hard through my chest, through my arms, up to my brain. It was bleeding within me, and I stepped forward into the space he had just been in, and he stepped back. I stepped forward, and he stepped back, and his eyes were empty bowls; something had spilled out of them. That's when I realized he was incredibly fucking scared.

"Run," I said, and he actually ran. He pumped his arms and everything. He disappeared in the direction of Marilynne's house, but at the time I just knew he was running away from me.

All of this made me feel a horrible neurochemical joy.

CHAPTER ONE

Maybe we could just keep on meeting like this forever. A whole book of Chapter Ones. We could always start anew. The world would keep beginning and beginning and beginning.

Try to stop it. You can't.

Okay, there's that way. But don't do it. Hang on.

CHAPTER ONE

I slid through the side door of the Replay out by the patio and then pushed up front to the bar. It wasn't last call yet, but they were counting down. A couple dozen people sopped up beer with their tongues. Uncle X and the smug, smug woman were long gone.

Casey's back was to me. I looked from the soft blond spikes on her head to her black boots and at everything in between, and I pressed my chest up against her back. I kissed down into the false violence of her hair.

"It's about fucking time," she said. She pushed over and created a little harbor for me next to the bar. I anchored there. We were pressed together between two inhabited stools. I didn't really look around. That wasn't on my mind.

I'd known Casey for a couple of years. Before I knew her, she had been a mess in high school out in the Kansas City suburbs, and her parents sent her to rehab and to Outward Bound, back and forth, until she got sick of it and stopped using. That was five years ago.

When I first met her, she had a black splotch, some strange dark birthmark, on the tip of her nose. It was bigger than a mole, smeary, and it was fascinating. It made her look even cooler and sadder and smarter—marked from birth to do something, maybe something epic, maybe not so epic but at least sort of interesting. I talked to her for hours, and when she came back from the restroom, she said, "Why didn't you tell me I had chocolate on my nose?"

That's when she was working at the chocolate place. She stole turtles from her employer to help rot my teeth. She was a waitress and graphic designer now, and she was always threatening to design a Neptune logo. "Like with a trident," she'd say.

I do not want—I will never want—a Neptune logo.

We slept together every few months, like band practice for a shitty punk group that will never play live, but, hey, we had some good songs, and you never know. She wanted to feel tough sometimes. She missed drugs. She wanted proximity to danger.

The dynamite hung on my back. The curve of Casey's hipbone pressed into my thigh.

"Sorry," I said "I had to take care of some Marilynne shit."

"Fun night?"

"The usual."

"Poor Neppy," she said, "the bluest planet." She kissed me right next to my mouth but not quite on it.

I signaled across the bar to Missy, the bartender, who nodded and poured me a beer.

"Hey," she said, "Calvin's looking for you. He called and asked if you were here."

"If he calls again—"

"No one is ever here," Missy said. "Ever."

"Did you step in dumb shit again?" Casey asked.

"Me?" I said. "Never."

"You have dumb shit all over you," Casey said. "You have blood on your pants!"

"It's Marilynne's," I said.

We layered beer over beer. I had whiskey somewhere in there too. We got all stratified.

So I had stolen some dynamite. So Calvin was pissed. So my phone kept spasming in my pocket. So Marilynne was hurting herself in new and fucked-up ways. None of these things seemed insurmountable.

"Do you want to see my backpack full of dynamite?" I asked Casey.

"Nice pick-up line," she said.

See: that's my problem. Even at my most earnest, she still thought I was full of shit.

Missy announced last call, and we fortified ourselves with shots of Jameson, beers to chase it. Casey's hand rested on the small of my back, right beneath the dynamite.

I kissed the top of her head again. I finished her beer.

Missy pointed at the door.

"Time to go, kids," Missy said.

"I think it had better be your place," I said to Casey.

CHAPTER ONE

I'm technically classified as a high-functioning drunkard.
The first step is admitting it.

CHAPTER ONE

Casey took me home. She had a little one-bedroom apartment on the second floor of a house on Ohio, up near campus. We wobbled there, kissed on street corners.

Inside, we kissed again, and then she planted her hands on my chest, pushed me away.

"Go take a shower," she said. "And take off that backpack."

I did not argue with her, even though I mainly just smelled like me, which would never come out, not even with the plastic vials of honey-smelling goop and extracted butterfly essence lined up along the rim of her bathtub.

I created a little shrine to Neptune: a bag full of dynamite and a pile of dirty jeans, a T-shirt, a hoodie that smelled like beer. I sat on the edge of the tub opposite the vials, breathed out junk and tried to breathe in something clean. I turned on the shower, ducked under, and scrubbed.

When I came out in a towel, she was fully clothed and lounging on her bed. She curled her index finger in toward me, then patted the bed.

"Let me touch you a little," she said.

I sprawled out next to her, and she ran a hand over my chest, down to my stomach, back up to my chest, down over my abs and then down to the towel. She ruffled my pubic hair and brushed her fingers along my inner thighs. She ran her hands over my Ad Astra tattoo. Her fingers were back on my chest, on my neck, near my penis, away from my penis, back along my abs, over my hip. I closed my eyes.

"This is torture," I said.

"Torture?"

"Exquisite torture."

"I haven't even started to torture you yet," she said, and then she started to take off her clothes.

I sat on the edge of the bed and watched. She shucked her jacket and smiled, and then she tugged off her boots, her socks, and frowned. As she pulled off her T-shirt, it got stuck on her chin and she laughed, and I looked at her bare breasts. When she freed herself, her spiky hair was wilder and softer and blowsy. She stood there topless and shoved her hand down the front of her skirt. Then she laughed and took two steps toward me, and she pulled out her hand, and she stuck a long wet index finger in my mouth.

"Suck it," she said, and I did, and I pulled down her skirt and her thong, and I kissed her belly button. I flipped her onto the bed, and she said, "Put your weight on me. No, grab a condom."

She kept going like that. She told me what to do, and I did it with teeth, with my tongue, with the tips of my fingers, and with the flat hard base of my hand. I stared at her breasts with my mouth. The entire room became skin. She tasted like sparks.

I woke up under her, needled and pinned, tingling and half erect again.

"Oh, man," she said, "I just fucked all the desire out."

"Yeah," I said, but I was lying. I still had desire. It had leached into my bones. I had desire all over the place.

I lied to her, but I'll never lie to you.

Her neck smelled like sweat and pink bubblegum. It wasn't quite morning, and a film of almost-day coated the room.

"I'm getting up for some water," I said, and she mumbled and rolled aside.

I had not yet entered hangover's domain. I was still drunk and giddy with blood. I pissed, and the circulation returned to the numb places, and I poured us two glasses of cold tap water.

She was up now. Eyes open but dreamily so.

"Water?"

"That's the nicest thing anyone's done for me today," Casey said.

I kissed the top of her hip, watched the line of her throat shift as she swallowed the water down.

"How long have we known each other?" Casey asked

"Maybe forever, or at least three years," I said.

She sat on my lap, naked her, my naked lap, and we listened to the ticking palpitations of each other's bodies. I could feel the blood flow back to my penis again. It pressed up against her flesh. Casey reached her hand between her legs, tunneled between us, and reached out to me.

"Hold on," she said. She made a fist around my penis. "This hurt?" she asked.

"Not really."

She squeezed harder.

"Not in a bad way," I said.

It felt raw and brutal and happy, and we sat that way for several minutes.

As we sat there in the watered-down light of dawn, stripped down to nothing, Marilynne appeared before the bed, and I knew it was a ghost. She looked at me with her moon face. She was unforgivably dead, and it made everything feel even flimsier and more important. Casey could break my penis off in her hand. Our flesh could shatter. Marilynne was dead, and she stared at us, an awful dented wound on the side of her face. She still wore that flowered dress, but she looked like an old duotone photograph, black and white and gray washed over with tints of blue. It made me think of hypothermia. She was entirely bruise.

"You see that."

"What?" Casey asked.

"Marilynne," I said. "She's here. She's a fucking ghost."

"Sure," Casey said, and she stroked me up and down, once hard and then once more gently. "It's a ghost."

"Oh, fuck," I said.

Marilynne just stood and stared. Her face looked stunted and pained, frozen.

"She's just going to have to watch us," Casey said.

She turned around and slipped me into her.

"I just need to feel all of you, living, nothing latex."

I could see Casey's eyes crinkle up. I could see Marilynne over her shoulder. She watched the whole time. It felt like a moment that demanded silence. We swallowed our moans.

CHAPTER ONE

I don't know when Marilynne disappeared. Casey laughed out loud, and she stretched her lips over her teeth, and she bit down over my eyelids one and then the other, and I had no choice but to close my eyes, just surrender to the blind wet tight aliveness. We sat there like that, and I listened to Casey's panting. I opened my eyes, looked around the room. There was more day and less Marilynne, none at all actually. I could feel my penis shrinking. I could feel the hangover getting hard.

"Kiss me," she said, and we kissed. Casey rolled off of me. "Maybe we can do that again before I have to go to work."

"Maybe," I said. I got up and grabbed my stuff from the bathroom and pulled on my pants. I said a silent *fuck you* to the backpack as I pulled it on.

"What are you doing?" she asked.

"I've got to see what's going on with Marilynne."

"What were you saying about all that shit?"

"What shit?"

"The ghost shit."

"I have this horrible feeling. I think she's dead."

"Whatever," she said. "I'm going back to sleep. I'm available for one more thorough fucking before nine."

"I'll be back," I said as I pulled open the door.

"Bring your ghost friend," she yelled. "She likes the way we do it."

The morning wore a bright fizzy glimmer. The sun was nearly up. I lit a cigarette and smoked it quick so the nicotine could buzz around my brain and counteract the hangover. The chemical sadness started to dig in. I licked my lips, and they tasted like Casey burnt at the stake. That's the kind of thing I thought. I moved my feet fast. I saw an old man with a dog, and the man waved, and the dog looked at me with a greedy, stupid look. I looked back the same exact way. I lit another cigarette.

When I got to Marilynne's house, it was cruel and full-on daylight, and the alcohol tremor stirred in my fingertips. It wanted to spread up my whole arm. I tried to spit it out of me, but I couldn't dredge up enough saliva. I spit on her lawn, and then I saw the door had been smashed open. The doorframe was in splinters. I felt a cold drip of something inside my guts.

She was sprawled face down on the living room floor.

CHAPTER ONE

I pushed my eyeballs up against the whole situation. Right from the start, it didn't look like sleep. It didn't look like being alive, but I wasn't thinking about deadness. Marilynne's face was slanted into the carpet, and her hair seemed pasted against her neck. Her skirt was pushed up, exposing her calves, which looked bruised. Her left leg no longer even looked like a leg. It was a long sack of broken blood vessels. She was bleeding into herself. Or she had bled herself out.

Her lungs didn't twitch, and a puddle of dark red souped in the rug under her face. I lay down on the floor next to her, didn't touch her, didn't think, didn't look at anything except the inside of my head.

"I'm so fucking sorry," I said. "I'm so fucking sorry. I'm so fucking sorry."

It delivered a strange comfort. That and the hangover centered me, gave me a switch of pain to beat my thoughts with.

I should have just called 911. That's what you say. That's what I say. But the me that's here right now isn't the me that was there. It was a different me. I flipped her over, and the left side of her face was cavity, absence. The cheek looked sunken. The left eye was no longer an eye. A mashed cornea, something that looked like cottage cheese, an eyelid ripped in half, a raw streak of blood turning black, a smell like sour milk, a fly tiptoeing on her and sucking on the open wound of her face. I almost slapped at it. The rest of her face was mottled with indentations from the carpet, like the tracks of worms. That might have been when I started to cry.

"I'm so fucking sorry," I said. "I'm so fucking sorry."

That's when I saw her again. The corpse still wore the oven mitt, but the ghost didn't. She stood over me, just watched me and her own desecrated face. She had the same bluish sheen. She looked like the kind of thing you could turn off with a remote control. We watched each other for a while.

I said, "I'm so sorry."

She didn't say a word.

CHAPTER ONE

In the kitchen, an electric iron sat in the sink next to a coffee cup and a whiskey glass. I picked up the iron. Strands of her gray hair were pasted to it with blood.

"Motherfucker," I said. The ghost Marilynne watched me all the while: as I cracked ice cubes out of a tray, as I shoveled them with my bare hand into a glass, as I poured in some whiskey, an inch, a half more for good measure, a splash extra for grace, a splash of water for health.

I called the police from the living room phone. Marilynne watched me as I watched her and her dead body.

"Hello," said the voice, feminine and weary, on the other end of the line

"There's been a murder," I said, and then I gave the address. I was a pithy motherfucker, and my stupidity was all over the place. My pants were stained with her blood, and my name was indelible, strung across the wall above us.

The whiskey spritzed away at the flame of hangover. The pain smoldered.

I thought about the cops and that motherfucker Tax. As if you didn't think of him too.

I stood there next to the corpse, drinking liquor that tasted like fingernail polish remover, lurking under the graffiti of my own name. I like to try to picture it from the ghost's perspective, from your perspective, from the cops'. I'd make some assumptions too.

I let myself out the back door and booked it over to New Jersey. I could sneak back to the apartment and tell Casey. I needed to tell someone, anyone.

I could see the ghost watching me from the backyard gate.

CHAPTER ONE

So I was sprinting up New Jersey, dawn all around me. That's when my phone rang. It was Marilynne's cell number, and for a whiskey-thin instant, I imagined she was alive. I imagined how everything that transpired, everything that died on me, could have been an elaborate practical joke, engineered for the entertainment of countless others, or at least countless Marilynnes, and, of course, for my spiritual enlightenment. (Today's lesson: Don't take others for granted, not even fucked-up and obnoxious others, or they will fake their own deaths and frame you for it, and then won't you be sorry? [You will.])

I wanted to believe. I wanted her live voice connected to a live body somewhere in the vast carbon-based universe.

"But you looked so dead," I said into the phone.

"This fucking Neptune?" a man asked. He bared his tone like teeth.

His pit-bull voice stretched to the end of its chain and lunged at my throat.

His voice sounded so harsh and thick and deep; all of it sounded fake.

"I know it's you, fucking Tax," I said.

He laughed like a jack o'lantern—hollowed out, something burning behind it.

"This ain't fucking Tax."

"You know him?"

He laughed again. Even more of it had been cut away.

"I'm trying to do you a solid," the voice said.

"What?"

"Don't go home."

I felt zapped by it, licked by it.

"Fuck you," I kicked back at it.

But the call had already clicked into the abyss.

"Fuck you," I yelled into the hole where communication dies, into my little piece of plastic and cadmium and coppery wire. I stood on the sidewalk before a pale blue house the color of pool water. The street had a feeling of coming alive. A few houses up, I could see a man in a suit going out to his car. Maybe I could catch a ride with him. He would loan me a suit. I would hide in his cubicle, crouching under the desk, and he would feed me crumbs of a glazed donut from the palm of his hand.

I didn't recognize the voice, its bark of a dog, its bark of a tree. That voice had texture and tack, like cigarette tar and canine slobber.

I couldn't go home anyway. I wondered if the anarchists would just kill someone like that or if fucking Tax would do something like that, and have I mentioned that almost everyone I love ends up dying?

And then I thought about Casey, curled up in her bed.

Oh shit, I thought. Shit shit shit.

I called Casey's cell.

After four, five, six rings, she said, "Hello?" She sounded pillowy, sleep sick.

"Something's gone down, Casey, like something bad."

"What do you mean?" She said it quickly, her voice suddenly tight and awake to the possibility of misery and my fuckheadedness.

"I don't know," I said, "and that makes it worse."

"What happened?" she asked. "Are you crying?"

"Marilynne's dead, and I think the police are coming for me."

I could hear police sirens revving up toward Marilynne's house two blocks away. I heard a chorus of them.

"You're kind of freaking me out," she said.

She hung up on me too.

CHAPTER ONE

Let's get some things straight:

* This is Kansas, but spare me the Oz jokes. (I will not tell Dorothy that you said hello.)

* Yes, I've heard the one about Uranus being the closest thing to Neptune.

* It's not because I have ADHD or anything. Sometimes I just want to start again.

* The ghost was really there.

CHAPTER ONE

A friend of mine, a guy named Jimmyhead, rented a little house on New York Street. I booked it there as fast as I could. I pounded up his porch and knocked on his door. Jimmyhead and I didn't hang out that much anymore.

"Hold on," he yelled from somewhere inside.

I listened to the empty call and response of carbon dioxide and oxygen, and I thought about when Jimmyhead used to be fun. One night we had kicked in the closet doors of his house, just to see who could do it with one kick—the answer, nobody. We had to kick those things until our shoelaces snapped. Another time we had an after-bars party there, and Jimmy said he woke up naked the next morning with all his doors and windows open and air blowing in and sunlight staring at his penis. He had slept on his couch under a portrait of Abraham Lincoln.

Old Abe looked after people like Jimmyhead. No one even stole his stereo that night.

When Jimmyhead finally opened the door, his long brown hair was slick and wet and he wore just an orange terry-cloth towel around his waist.

"Don't you ever wear clothes anymore?"

We both looked down at his towel. It had a couple of bleach spots.

"What's the frequency, Kenneth?" he asked.

I almost called him Jimmyhead, which he didn't like anymore, and then I said, "Jimmy, I need a place to crash."

He gave me a shit monkey look and then waved me inside. I sat on his couch under the photo of Abe Lincoln. Abe knew I was naked under those clothes. He knew I had sinned. Wasn't I a man? That dude knew sin was part of the ground rules.

Jimmyhead came back wearing chinos and a collared shirt.

"What did you do now?" he asked.

"I've got some bad news, man."

He sat down across from me. His face wrinkled up around the corners of his mouth and at the ridges of his eyes. He knew Marilynne too. She had introduced us at some party, back when she threw parties.

"Marilynne's dead," I said.

He wasn't surprised by this at all, but he looked old all of a sudden. The skin around his eyes formed tight papery gullies, and he gathered his long brown hair behind his head, gave it a yank as if he were trying to start his brain via pull cord. He pulled on his hair again, and then he cried a little bit.

"She was a good lady," he said.

"She was," I said, and the Marilynne ghost and Honest Abe both watched us. Jimmyhead rubbed his eyes and nose with the cuff of his shirt.

"And, man," I said, "the cops are going to think I did it."

He gave me a hard knot of a look, then held it.

"Did you kill her?" he asked. His quiet voice slithered between us. "Is that her blood on your pants?"

"Fuck no," I said, "you fucking asshole fuckhead."

He looked at me some more.

"It would have been the worst thing you've ever done," he said flatly.

"I didn't do it."

The three of them looked at me. The portrait of Abe Lincoln seemed the most alive.

"I see her everywhere," I said.

"She was kind of like a mother to you, wasn't she?"

"She was the fucked-up Freudian mother I never had."

I tried to tell him the whole story. I told him everything I told you, except for the intimate details of my anatomy. The rest is for everyone, but only you are allowed the privilege of touching my comma scab.

"That's a fucked-up story," he said. "You're the most fucked-up person I know."

Jimmyhead brought me a cold can of Miller Lite and a big mug of dirt-black coffee.

"I'm letting you stay for a while because I'm your stupid asshole friend."

I drank from the beer and then the coffee and then tried to bludgeon the tang of both with more beer.

"If I find out you did it," he said, "you're fucking dead."

CHAPTER ONE

Jimmyhead had to go to work.

I called Casey on my cellphone, and she didn't pick up, and she didn't pick up again, and she didn't pick up another time. I actually thought *I should call Marilynne*, and then I remembered. Maybe I cried for a while.

I found another bleach-stained towel, and I took a long hot shower. I wanted to turn into steam. I figured I had better wait until nightfall to go looking for Tax.

Jimmyhead owned about two hundred books, including all of Marilynne's. Here's what she wrote in one of them:

> Dear Jimmyhead,
> It's the stupidest name ever for the stupidest, sweetest man.
> > With much love,
> > Marilynne

I didn't want to read her books, not even her inscriptions. I didn't want to read Kafka. I didn't want to read anything that seemed to be about anything. But every single book I started seemed to want to create meaning.

I bet you didn't even think I could read (but I can). I thought about that "Don't Go Home" note in *Great Expectations*, and let's just say that some of the Lawrence cops were familiar with who I was. Maybe I should have told you some stuff earlier, but it didn't seem important at the time.

Jimmyhead didn't have *Great Expectations*, but he had *David Copperfield*.

I read the words "I am born," and then I read that first line about whether or not Copperfield will be the hero of his own life, and then I thought, who wants to read a book about a fucking orphan? I slayed David Copperfield on the spot.

And, yes, I know what Holden Caulfield said about all that Copperfield crap. Of course I've read *The Catcher in the Rye*. If you haven't, put this book down and go read *The Catcher in the Rye*.

Then I saw that Jimmyhead had a copy of *Huck Finn*. I had never read it before, and that suddenly seemed fucked up and sad.

I sniffed the book. It smelled slightly minty and oaky the way certain books do, and I ruffled the pages, which were still tight and new and crisp, and I wanted to stay there in that moment, but it passed. I could feel Marilynne's ghost scrutinizing me.

It was a cheap-ass paperback, the absolute best kind of book. When you drop those fuckers in the bathtub, they mushroom out to twice the size. That's a bonus for you, twice the absolute mass. You can squish those things into a jacket pocket. You can lose them on the bus. Books were made for shit like that. They are the friends you can absolutely rip apart. Snap their spines and see if they care.

Try it with this one. Bend this motherfucker back. Flip ahead to 209 and dog-ear the page. You'll get to it later. It will be worth it—I promise. You'll get there and you'll think, I should have believed good old Neptune. But that's between you and me. (I'll be checking page 209 for your dog-ear, by the way.) This was between me and Huck and fucking Abe Lincoln and poor dead Marilynne gawping away. I had no idea if they wanted me to read the book or not, but *Huck Finn* looked like the kind of thing that could crush your brain for a while. What else was I going to do? Pray? I needed to squish my gray matter because my neurons kept running back to Marilynne's house and finding her and telling me not to pick up the iron as I picked up the iron. Was it hot when it bashed in her face? As if that could have made any of it any worse.

On the inside front cover, I wrote *Property of Neptune*. Then for good measure I also wrote it on page 43. Then I started from the beginning, the only way to recreate the world.

CHAPTER ONE

I consider reading a form of prayer. And you should too. You'd feel holier already.

Even reading this piece of shit would classify as spirit work.

Bless you, pilgrim. Bless you.

CHAPTER ONE

I don't know why I was reading, to be honest.

Maybe you're thinking the same fucking thing.

Sometimes that shit just happens.

I stayed there all day, drinking Jimmyhead's Miller Lite and reading *Huck Finn* and frying up the last of his bologna and eating it on stale white bread. I washed my jeans in the bathroom sink, pummeling them with bar soap, scrubbing the bloodstains from red down to pink and finally a funny tan blur that wouldn't surrender. Those pants would never just be jeans again. I sat on the edge of the tub and transformed them from soaking wet to a cloying dampness with Jimmyhead's hair dryer. When I tried to put them back on, I felt like a burn victim, swaddled in something cool and weird and medicinal. Maybe nothing would feel comfortable ever again. Maybe the jeans were fine and it was my skin that would be fucked up and clammy forevermore.

You would have had the same cockeyed thoughts, just in some different way.

Or maybe you wouldn't have even tried to pull those wet pants back up your legs.

Probably you wouldn't have ended up in a situation like this. If you ever do, I'd recommend drying them in a microwave. You can watch the rivets and buttons spark.

Jimmyhead didn't have a microwave. He barely had beer. I shed those pants. I read the book in my boxer shorts.

"What?" I said, and the ghost didn't say anything at all.

CHAPTER ONE

Although parts of this book may seem flippant, none of this stuff felt flippant at the time. I'm kind of glad I can't recreate the sadness. It was bad enough once.

It's not that kind of mystery; I can tell you who did it right now if you want.

Maybe by now, you have your own "theories." Maybe I warned you about them. Maybe you're absolutely fucking sure you know who did it.

Maybe you consider me something worse than a liar. I've been called worse things. I'm used to all that.

Think all you want. It's probably good practice for you.

That's when I finally remembered my phone.

Maybe you would have checked your phone right away. But maybe you're intent on solving a crime. Maybe you check it all the time.

I listened to my messages.

Calvin at 12:05 a.m.: "Just bring it back, dude."

Calvin at 12:06 a.m.: "Bring it back now, the stuff."

Calvin at 12:07 a.m.: "I'm getting kind of pissed, asshole."

Calvin at 12:33 a.m.: "All right, Neptune, real fucking funny. Just bring it back now."

Calvin at 1:15 a.m.: "Just bring it back and there's no problem. I mean it."

Calvin at 1:18 a.m.: "You are one of the top three stupidest motherfuckers I've ever met. You are fucked six ways to Wednesday."

Calvin at 1:20 a.m.: "I mean it: you're dead. When we find you, you're dead."

Marilynne at 2:05 a.m.: "Neptune, pick up. Pick up! Pick up. Some men were here looking for you. They broke down my door, kicked it in. They owe me a new door. You owe me a new door. They want you and your backpack. That door was beautiful, you know. Get here as soon as you can."

Marilynne at 2:06 a.m.: "Those men are gone now. I should have said that."

Marilynne at 2:07 a.m.: "They said you stole something. I don't like the police, but that's not why I'm not calling the police. Get here as soon as you can."

Marilynne at 2:08 a.m.: Just the click of someone hanging up.

Calvin at 2:15 a.m.: "The old lady said you were there. That bitch's as fucked up as you are. We trashed your apartment too."

Calvin at 2:16 a.m.: "In case you were wondering, you're still dead."

Marilynne at 2:43 a.m.: She didn't say hello. Just: "Help. Help please."

It boiled just over the level of whisper.

"What the fuck are you doing, bitch?" a voice yelled, and then Marilynne said, "Stay back" in a steady, normal voice, and then a "Stay back" strained through a tight, narrow opening, a keyhole peering into fear, and then I heard a gruff "Fucking bitch," and then I heard a loud wet clapping sound.

Oh, Christ, I thought. I played it back, listened to her die again.

"What the fuck are you doing, bitch?"

It was loud, slurred. It was a black and blue voice. It was made out of tar. It stuck to your ears. It was the man-dog's voice.

I listened to her die again. The "Stay back" was so calm and then so terrified.

Of all the things to do, she called me.

The clapping sound was deep and hollow. I could hear her blood. I could feel the steamed scorch of iron kissing the fabric of her: skin and fat, muscle and bone.

The Marilynne ghost watched me as she died over and over on the phone. I listened until my left eyelid twitched, and then I listened some more.

Each time I listened, I wondered: did they kill her because of me?

CHAPTER ONE

There were a lot more messages from Calvin telling me what flavor of dead I was.

I called Marilynne's cell, but all I got was her recorded voice saying, "Never ever leave a message."

Whoever stole it might not even have it anymore. How about that for detective work?

Even I had to create some form of organization. I gave each of the numbers—Calvin, the bark-voiced man—a different ring tone. The phone would ring, and I could say, *Oh, it's Marilynne's murderer.*

I did not get cute. None of them were "Sympathy for the Devil."

If the phone made a short rude moan, it was the killer.

That's how you'll know when a killer calls for you.

I bet your phone has a murderer setting too.

CHAPTER ONE

I stewed in my own sadness. I studied the trajectory of guilt. I read the book.

I considered giving you pages and pages about my own reading: a list of pages I dog-eared, phrases I underlined, how I sometimes stopped and thought about all the horrible stuff that had happened, how I stopped and looked around for the ghost, how I sometimes saw her (just watching me), how I sometimes unzipped the backpack to count the sticks of dynamite (always six), how I sometimes thought about checking my phone and then stopped myself, the way I got to know Huck, the way I got to know Jim, the way I held the book with one hand and sometimes picked my nose with the other or scratched as far as I could down between my shoulder blades. I ate Jimmyhead's snacks, such as they were, bologna-based mostly.

Instead, let's talk about the past.

As you excavate my ancient shit, layers and layers of it, I'll just be sitting here reading a book. We'll catch up with me later.

CHAPTER ONE

Actually I'm not sure I can get into all of that shit right now.

Let's just say that everyone who was supposed to love me died or went crazy, sometimes both.

After all that, you'd want people to keep their distance.

It's not that I don't like other humans. I don't trust other humans.

I don't trust myself. I've done the stupidest stuff ever, and I keep doing it. How can you count on people when they do that?

What if I wake up in the morning, all hungover and destroyed and ready for something different, and then by 10 p.m. I'm doing the same exact shit I did the night before? What if I wake up proclaiming never again, and then the cycle repeats?

Now do you see why I don't trust myself? You probably don't trust me either.

I've seen how you look at some of these pages. I know what you skim, how you blanched while touching my comma. I didn't even ask you to stroke it.

Do you see how that verb changes everything? It's not that kind of comma.

CHAPTER ONE

We haven't even gotten to the Ghost Machine. We haven't even gotten to Saskia.

Whether she's to be the fucking hero of my life or not, let these pages decide. Isn't there some book that goes like that?

If I'm not the hero, I must be my own antagonist. It makes life a hell of a lot harder.

The Ghost Machine's pretty fucked up, by the way.

I warned you.

I warned you so many pages ago, back when you had the chance to quit without feeling guilty about it. You're in too deep now.

Keep going.

CHAPTER ONE

I was just sitting there, minding my own business, reading a book, just like you're doing. Then my phone palsied. It was a number I didn't know. The phone had been convulsing every ten minutes actually, and I tried to ignore it, all the its: the voicemails, the texts, the portal to the fucking Internet. The phone was plugged in, filling itself with juice.

Maybe the police somehow had my number?

I don't even know why I picked it up. All these voices were coming for me, wanted to shriek at me, and, still, every time that phone buzzed, did its little mechanical shimmy like a bug electrified and stuck on its back, I had to look.

In my ear, someone said, "Neptune?"

I knew it right away: a woman's voice, a little breathy and a little husky. It had a resonant quality to it, like it echoed out of an ancient throat.

I was listening to it still, even during the pause when I was, I guess, supposed to speak, so she said it again: "Neptune?"

"Yeah," I said.

"I need to see you," she said.

I knew who it was. I could imagine parts of her.

She sounded like her brother, even though she didn't really sound like him. I had heard her voice only a couple of times, maybe only that one time for any extended period.

"It's Saskia," she said.

"I know," I said.

"Allen's sister. I'm the one—"

"I know."

"Allen's dead, you know. Someone shot him a year ago."

"I heard that," I said. Marilynne's ghost stood before me, slumped a little around the shoulders, like her hands were heavy, a tired boxer.

"I've got to ask you something really weird," she said.

"What?"

"Do you remember the Ghost Machine?" she asked.

"Not really," I said, but then I did: all of a sudden, I remembered Allen rigging it up—an old Sony Walkman—and paying some kind of medicine person, both woman and man or neither, who was said to be 150 years old, to fill it with enchantment. Allen drove all the way across Kansas to get the spell, the blessing, the curse, the whatever. He paid two hundred bucks. He wanted a machine to call up his old ghosts. He wanted to see a dead girlfriend he had loved more than anything, and his mother, and he hoped he'd get to see this Doberman named Ice, who licked up a green puddle of antifreeze and died. That dog didn't even belong to him. This magic Walkman, he called it the Ghost Machine. Of course it didn't work. He threatened to drive all the way back across Kansas and fuck up that Indian's world.

I remembered then, too, that the Walkman had actually been mine. I loaned it to him, or maybe he just took it. I don't know why he used my Walkman. I don't know why he believed any of that shit.

"Are you there?" she asked. "Are you seeing anything weird?"

"It's really fucked up," I said, "but I can see a ghost."

"I knew it!" she said. "It started running last night, all by itself. I could hear it playing in a box of Allen's old stuff."

"How'd you get my number?" I asked.

"Allen had it. He kept tabs on you. He wrote down places where you lived, phone numbers."

"He fucked me over," I said, "and then he did it again."

"I know," she said. "He said it was the worst thing he'd ever done."

I didn't say anything.

"Can you see my brother? Can you see his ghost?"

"I can't," I said.

"I'm still coming to see you," she said. "I want to see the ghost, to see if I can see him."

I hardly knew her at all. Her brother had been like my brother, and then a bunch of bad shit happened, and he became this anti-brother. Saskia and I didn't even know each other, not really, and we already had this fucked-up little history. We were intimate in this fucked-up way.

There's a story I'll probably have to tell you.

I had too much to process already.

I tried to squiggle out a to-do list in my head.

   1. *Dispose of the dynamite*
   2. *Find Tax*
   3. *Get rid of the ghost*

Like, why couldn't number three be number one? Shouldn't I get rid of the ghost first? Couldn't Saskia help me? Did all of this start with the Ghost Machine?

"Are you there?" she said. "I can hear you breathing."

I told her to meet me at Harbour Lights, a bar down on Mass Street, in an hour. Some part of me didn't trust her. Some part of me wanted other people around.

Of course I believed her. I'd been seeing ghosts since page 54.

CHAPTER ONE

I know the tone and the voice and the mood of this book, the conflict and the central plot, the fucking style, the style of fucking, change every page and a half.

Imagine if that shit happened all the time in your regular life. I bet you'd write a cogent and consistent narrative then.

If I had been trying to "detect" anything, we would have been "uncovering" "clues," "interrogating" "suspects," "analyzing" "quotation marks." I didn't do any of this. The gravitational force that pulled me toward books, toward liquor, would magnetize Tax eventually too, and if the cops found me, they found me. I could have been found anywhere. I was always someplace. It might as well be Harbour Lights.

CHAPTER ONE

I left a note for Jimmyhead: *I owe you. I know it. I'm sorry. I'm probably coming back to crash.*

I went into the bathroom and pulled on my jeans. They were dry but stiff, cardboardy. I had to bend my knees a few times to loosen things up.

I called work and let them know I wasn't coming in.

You probably didn't think I'd be that conscientious.

You probably thought I didn't even have a job, but I always work like a motherfucker. Back then, I worked the door at a slick, corny new bar out on Twenty-Third, one I would never go to as a patron, one I hate to even name, but they paid me well, and besides, all the bars I used to work the door for decided my services weren't strictly necessary anymore. I helped a guy install under-the-table carpet jobs. I did all kinds of work for Marilynne.

Do you know I have my GED, that I'm a college dropout?

Have I shown you my comma scab?

Do you need to see references?

CHAPTER ONE

When I entered Harbour Lights, Joey the bartender looked up, frowned.

"Some dudes are looking for you," he said.

"Anarchist dudes?"

"Yep."

"Pretend I'm not here."

"I don't want any shit in here today," he said. "I'm hungover."

"Bad?"

"Death via percussion."

"If any of Calvin's dudes come in, I'm gone."

"And if the cops come?"

So he knew. I guess everybody knew.

"Same deal," I said.

The police were looking for me. I was a person of interest, which sounds flattering if you take it out of context.

"If it makes you feel any better," he said, "I don't think you did it. Not even you are stupid enough to be walking around under those circumstances."

He poured me a pint without asking and then a shot of whiskey for both of us.

"This'll put the hair of the dog on your chest," he said.

We drank the kind burn of it.

"Better?" I said.

"Better," he said.

Harbour Lights is a huge long room, like a humongous brick shoebox, and Joey and I were mice sniffing around in it. It reeked of the sweetness of spilled beer and the odor of things about to catch fire.

The place was nearly empty. Two older townies played pool. I checked my phone: 4 p.m.

She'd be there soon.

CHAPTER ONE

I don't know what she was wearing. I can't tell you if it had pleats.

I'm pretty sure she wore clothing.

I'm pretty sure I would've noticed if she hadn't. That would have stuck with me, I suspect.

When Saskia walked into Harbour Lights, she reminded me of potato chips and a grilled cheese sandwich and a girl sitting on my lap when I was fifteen years old.

Saskia grabbed my hands. Both of them, not like a handshake but like the prelude to some kind of dance. It was a weird thing to do. She looked up into my face, and I looked down into hers, and she had this sliver of her brother in the shape of her forehead, the set of her eyes, which were too bright to be his, too methodical—maybe even scientific. She had eyes like the first bright blue flame of a gas stove.

"Boo," Saskia said, and I said, "Very funny," or something like that. I remember every word I said, except for maybe those ones.

"Let me look at you," she said.

"No," I said up to the ceiling. It was a tall one; prehistoric nicotine stained the upper walls, from the days when you could smoke in bars and every bartender had lung cancer and a really nice lighter. Nobody scrubbed up there. Nobody looked up there, which made the scrubbing unnecessary.

I was thinking about stuff like that when she grabbed my face and pulled it down a little.

"You've looked at me," she said.

I looked at her hard, and she looked back.

"Harder," she said, and for a beat, I thought she could read my thoughts. It could have happened. It's that kind of story.

"What?" I said.

"This is harder than I thought."

"I'm not going to hug you."

"I don't want you to hug me," she said. Maybe that's what the hand-grabbing was all about. She held them down by our sides. It created this buffer zone of air between us that we could send words back and forth through. Her hands reminded me of the seashell-shaped bars of soap Marilynne put out in her bathroom. I always had some shit to wash off my hands. I was afraid to use those soaps. Once I touched them, they'd be ruined.

She held my hands like that for a while, long enough that it became a question of dominance. I tried to let go and she held on.

"Do you miss him?" she said.

"Who?"

"My brother." She said it loud, and her voice opened some kind of fissure in the word *brother*. Some undergrads by the bar were looking over, and I gave them a fuck-off glare.

I didn't think I did at first, but, no, I did. I missed everybody.

"Yeah," I said.

Ghosts are not a substitute for humans. Thoughts are not a substitute for ghosts. Fucked-up memories are not a substitute for thoughts.

She held my hands and summoned up all these fucked-up memories.

She leaned in close and whispered, "Tell me about the ghost. Tell me everything."

Her mouth hovered right by my ear. "Everything," she said, and then she turned and offered her ear up to my mouth.

"I don't know anything," I said right into her head.

She pulled away but still held on. "I knew you'd say that," she said in a normal voice. "Allen always said you acted like you didn't know shit, but you do know shit. It was half a joke."

"Maybe a quarter," I said.

She leaned back in and whispered again. The little broken hairs in my ear canal danced for her. "I have the Ghost Machine," she said. "It's in my purse. It's on. It's been running, and I can't shut it off."

CHAPTER ONE

She couldn't see her brother's ghost. She couldn't even see Marilynne's.

"Tell me about the ghost," she said, and I tried. I described the ghost to her just like I described it to you.

"Why the fuck did Allen want the Ghost Machine anyway?" she said, and I told her about the dead Doberman, about his dead girlfriend.

"But the big fucking question is, why is it working for me?" I said.

She didn't know either.

Maybe Allen actually made it for me. Maybe he knew I was the kind of person who needed people to come back.

She pulled out the Walkman. Allen had sealed part of it with duct tape, and he had written GHOST MACHINE across the tape in black ballpoint pen. "See," she said, "it works." Sure enough, the spindles were churning. "I think it summons ghosts. It summons your ghosts."

"Can you stop it?" I asked,

She hit stop, but it whirred on. She hit eject, but the door wouldn't open.

"It might never shut off," she said. "You might see ghosts for the rest of your life."

Marilynne stood over us. I picked at the duct tape with my fingernail, and Saskia slapped my hand.

"Put on the headphones," she said. They were the ancient kind, with decomposing foam pads and a metal band that tiara-ed your head.

I slipped them on, and I heard a crackle, some static awakening, and then I heard my voice. I recognized it as my voice even as it seemed estranged from my existence, from my belief in my voice. It wasn't higher or lower. I don't know what it was.

"You're not KKK anymore," I said. "You're not anything. You're not dead because of me."

"This is my curse," a woman's voice said. "I will come back —"

I ripped off the headphones.

"This is fucked up," I said. "It's playing part of my life."

"I know," Saskia said. "It plays all different parts."

"Did you listen to this?"

"Some," she said. "A lot actually."

She had to know me better than anyone. The Ghost Machine sliced me open like a watermelon. You could see the red flesh of me, all the little black marks, all those little bad seeds.

"And?" I said.

"I'm sorry," she said.

"For listening?"

"For what happened to you," she said.

I didn't say anything for a while. We stared at each other until she shrugged.

"You recorded all of that shit on the cassette," she said.

"The fuck I did."

"Who did it, then?"

"It's weird," I said. "Someone taped it all, but it wasn't me. I'd never want to hear that again."

"The tape's jammed in there or something. Your whole life is jammed in there."

I looked at her, this small tough thing. Saskia was like the lever on a car jack: just this thin piece of metal, but it can lift the entire car. I think she'd like that. I think it has to do with physics.

Would you want someone to listen to all of that, all of the things that happened to you, recorded in stereo?

You can probably imagine your own Ghost Machine, your own ghost. Maybe the one who loved you the most would come back to you, even if you didn't love that person enough, even if that love got ruined somehow.

Maybe it doesn't have anything to do with love.

If you listen long enough to my Ghost Machine, you can hear long stretches of me saying weird bullshit over and over.

And, yes, I can see how maybe it's a metaphor for this book.

It replayed bad parts, good ones, strange boring ones. Lots of people had yelled at me, I guess.

I could listen to that thing forever. I never wanted to listen to it again.

The Ghost Machine made a clunking sound, and then it whirred again.

I heard a screaming argument between me and some girl when I was fifteen. I can't even remember her name. We didn't use names when we yelled at each other.

Then the machine clunked again, whirred again.

I heard Allen on the day he met me.

"Dude," he said, "I've got a place you can stay. My couch is your couch."

"You sure?" I said.

"Motherfucking sure as shit," he said, and then I remember that we shook hands, and he pulled me in, this strange and dangerous hug.

Clunk. Whir.

"I'm doing you up right," Allen said.

I could hear the buzz of the clippers, and then I yelped, "Shit, man."

I remembered how the clippers had bit away at the tip of my right ear as he shaved my head.

"I did that on purpose," Allen said. "A little blood never hurts."

I remembered clumps of my hair fluttering down to dirty gray linoleum.

CHAPTER ONE

I had one live ghost and the voices of all these others.

"Tell me more about her," Saskia said. I tried. You can't just pin ghosts down like butterflies.

Who would want to pin down butterflies? I have inflicted great pain, but I almost never murder a living thing.

It's not like I introduced myself as a choirboy. I don't think so anyway. You could go back and check if you want. I'll wait here.

CHAPTER ONE

I guess I should tell you about the before. I guess I should tell you about some of the shit.

I guess I should tell you what happened with Allen, with Saskia, with the skinheads.

And maybe I should explain that these skins aren't what you're thinking. They were "safety skins," anti-racist, anti-corporate. They're harmless really, violent as all get-out, but harmless. I wasn't involved, not fully. I went to some parties. I shaved one guy's head until his nubbly, pink flesh appeared. It was startling. He looked kind and soft and fresh, tender. That's up close, but I've seen this guy pull a Mike Tyson on somebody. I'm not kidding. I heard the ring of ear cartilage crack between his teeth. I heard the other man screaming, high and tight, in some molecular language. No one understands it anymore, but that language is our only true way of discussing pain. We can speak it. We just can't comprehend.

The skins understand the power of that transaction.

If the skins were walking down the street, you'd cross and walk on the other side.

And, okay, fine: I was involved. I lived with them. I shaved heads. I shaved my own down to the bristle-rasp stubble that comes when your hair barely exists. I was a not-quite skinhead.

When I shaved off my hair, I felt like something new, like some-one else. You would too. Try it. An electric razor costs about fifteen bucks. Self-transformation should cost a hell of a lot more than that.

I shaved heads, and I punched shitheads, and I kicked some ribs until they cracked. If I had told you this on page four, what would have happened to the two of us? I'm a violent asshole, but you can kill me on the spot. If you put this book down, I die. Pick it up, and I live again. You have some crazy God juice in your veins right now. I myself killed off Huck Finn, resurrected him, condemned him to die, saved him again. Feel free to do the same to me. I can take it.

Just promise to come back and resurrect me.

So I was fully involved with the skins. We weren't quite aligned with the anarchists, but if you drew a Venn diagram, we'd be humping each other's legs. We got involved in some serious shit. We had beat up a couple of Ku Klux Klan motherfuckers from Topeka, and a few times we went into Kansas City and threw down with some bikers who were fucking with some Muslim students. It was a delicate balance, an egg wobbling on a table: principles and violence. We beat the shit out of racists.

We threw some great fucking parties too.

CHAPTER ONE

You still there?

CHAPTER ONE

And then we had another run-in with the KKK. We were heading into Kansas City to beat the shit out of those people. I guess I need to tell you about this in particular.

We were safety skins, or you might have heard us being called SHARPs. It's not exactly an official thing. No dues, no uniforms—okay, sure, the heads are kind of a uniform.

But you have a head too.

I was seventeen years old. I was even callower than I am now. I was even dumber than I am now, if that's even possible.

Allen and I had been fighting over this girl. He didn't want to sleep with her anymore, but he didn't want anyone else to sleep with her either.

Her name was Tomorrow. I'm not joking. I don't remember much about her. It makes me a little sad.

CHAPTER ONE

Allen left to borrow a truck, and then he came to pick me up at the skins' house. I knew he was pissed at me. I knew this trip wasn't going to be fun.

Allen wanted maximum violence. We were going to Kansas City to perpetrate it, to perpetuate it.

I could hear the nothing of outside coming in through the window, and then I heard the rumble of the truck. The muffler muffled nothing. Allen wanted you to know when he arrived.

He hit the horn twice, real fast, and then again and held it.

I could have pretended I wasn't there, but how long would he have waited, how many times would he have hit the horn? Each one would have been a scold, a way of saying *coward*.

If I ended up killing someone, it was just something that had to happen. I remember thinking this as I slammed the front door behind me.

I walked down to the truck, cracked the passenger door. Allen pointed behind him, said, "In the back."

I could have sat up front at least until he picked up the others. I could have walked right back inside the house.

Instead, I hoisted myself over the tailgate, huddled up against the back of the cab.

Allen slid open the little window between the cab and the bed.

"Ready?" he said.

"Fuck you," I said, and he closed the window, nodded through the glass.

He drove like he wanted to double the wind.

The cold tried to kiss my legs through my jeans. The truck bed was scraped down to bare metal, flecks of rust, worn stripes of the original red paint. So much shit had been shoved into that pickup and then out again. I could see the fog of my breath as we whistled through the cold street. I had an ax handle wrapped with electrical tape. I had a four-inch buck knife, sharp enough to Van Gogh somebody. I had never cut anyone with it. It was too knifelike to use in that way. I wanted to go home and butter toast with it, an English muffin.

On the way to Kansas City, we picked up a few other skins, and we picked up a German Shepherd, relegated like me to the back.

As we sped down the highway toward Kansas City, that German Shepherd and I found a mutual interest in staying warm.

CHAPTER ONE

We hung out all day and drank beer in someone's apartment in Kansas City, and at about 10 p.m., we drove down to a city park, where the Klan was having a rally. Six people in sheets were spewing up bullshit near a fountain in this decrepit park. One of the sheets hollered before a little campfire. There was no audience. It was some fucked-up private ceremony, an initiation or something.

My ax handle was gone. I had this great capacity for losing things.

"A little violence never hurt anyone," Allen said.

Allen started yelling as we walked toward the park, and then he threw a bottle, drilled it right into the campfire. Flames rushed out, and we ran at those assholes. There were at least ten of us, all shaved down to scalps.

Those assholes scattered. I chased after one of those sheets, ran like a motherfucker.

We headed out of the park and across a major street and then into a rundown neighborhood.

I pumped my arms and sprinted. The man under the sheet was slow. I was gaining. I was so close I could hear his breath, a hot and frequent gasp. Above us, the sky was dark gray.

He ran down an alley, but I ran faster. When I got close enough, I kicked out at the back of his left knee, and it made me stumble, but he buckled and released this high, awful moan, and then my momentum plowed into him. My weight pushed him toward the tar and we fell together. Something made a cracking sound as his hand hit the ground, and I thought, *finger bone*, and I pictured a piece of chalk snapping, something I wished I had done up in front of a blackboard, back when there were blackboards to be embarrassed in front of.

I had a Kluxer under me. I pulled back on the sheeted head, and then I slammed his forehead into the pavement, and the voice said, "Stop," and it was a female voice.

I straddled her and flipped her over. I ripped off the hood, and a bloody forehead with eyes stared back at me.

"We could fuck," she said, "right here."

I spit in her face, and then I tried to summon up more saliva to do it again. Her arms were pinned by my legs, and the spit rolled down from the bridge of her nose toward her eye.

She said, "I will bear your children. They will be pure. I can purify you."

I spit again, and it hit her other eye.

"I'm not pure," I said. I wrapped my hands around her neck.

A neck is firm and strong. It feels ropy. It feels like a plastic flowerpot, under the flesh I mean. You can break that plastic if you apply enough torque.

(I bet you wish I had stopped and recognized the poverty of my own act. I bet you wish I had seen the tragedy of my own actions, my failure as a human being, the emptiness of all this.)

(Or maybe you're sort of rooting for me?)

I could smell urine. I ripped the sheet right off her.

"You're not KKK anymore," I said. "You're not anything. You're not dead because of me."

"This is my curse," she said. "I will come back in your women. I will come back. You will see me in your daughters. You will see me when your wife parts her legs. You will see me in your mother."

"I don't have a mother," I said.

I left her there in her pissed jeans.

She would do all kinds of evil thinking. That would continue, and I knew it. She would pray for the eradication of brown babies, black babies, yellow babies.

This is my almost-murder. I could have killed her. I don't think I would have lost any sleep.

I didn't like that I had touched her. I didn't like that she had felt my fluids.

My spit was in her eye, part of her.

CHAPTER ONE

In the alley in Kansas City, I committed murder in my mind. She knew this. I left the idea of her dead.

She yelled at me as I walked away: "Rapist chink, rapist chink, chink fucker, chink rapist."

She could turn adjectives into nouns and back again, which is what I think about now, but then my brain felt like bloody mud. I thought about running back and kicking her until her meat was ground, until her teeth littered the alley, until she shut up for five minutes or forever.

My own fingernails bit into the palms of my hands. I raised my own blood, and I walked away as she screamed and screamed, "Fucking chink."

I wandered back to the park, but everyone was gone. I heard sirens, and I wandered some more.

After everything, we were going to meet at some bar, and I had to ask this random fucker in a suede blazer how to get there.

"Four blocks," he said, and he pointed, and he lied, except for his finger, because the direction was right, but it was ten blocks, maybe more. I had to ask three more people, and one said, "You're bleeding," and I saw it dripping off my palm. That's how I read my palm: four self-induced crescent moons filling with blood.

When I got to the bar, a beard attached to a fat guy asked for my ID, and I said, "I'm here with Stevie K.," and he waved me in. Everyone was drinking in the back.

Someone handed me a beer, and someone handed me a shot, and someone handed me another beer. I drank myself into oblivion, but it took a while.

"I made mine piss her pants," I said. "It was a woman."

"Bad luck," Allen said. "Hitting a woman, I mean."

CHAPTER ONE

I woke up in the back of the pickup truck, stars for a quilt, wind running through my skin and deep into my bones and then into the marrow, which *wouldn't* freeze, which *could* get eaten up. But you have to snap the bones first. You have to break them to get to the good part.

I felt whole, cold but whole.

I didn't know where the German Shepherd was. I didn't know who was driving, I had to peek into the cab to make sure it was the right truck.

Allen was driving, and two women I didn't recognize were lined up next to him. His right hand was tucked between the thighs of the one pushed up next to him. We were on a highway but not I-70—there weren't enough lanes. We weren't headed for home, at least not yet.

We drove into the night. We were going some way, and it didn't matter to me that I didn't know which one.

I woke up wind-drunk. I woke up into motion. Allen was driving that truck hard. We had somewhere to go, I was sure of it.

I thought that bad luck would just blow right past me.

CHAPTER ONE

I rapped on the cab. Allen rolled down his window.

"What?" he yelled, and it blew back to me.

"I'm going to freeze back here," I said.

"Too bad," he yelled, and he rolled up the window, but he finally pulled over into the shoulder, and I jumped out. The passenger door opened.

"Get in," the gal said, and I pushed in next to her. She smelled like skin and cigarettes. We were jammed together. She grabbed hold of my knee.

"It doesn't mean anything," she said. "I've got to hold onto something or I feel all wobbly."

"You were passed out back there," Allen said.

"Snoring even," the other woman said.

The one I was pressed into said "I'm Emma" right into my ear.

"Where are we going?" I said.

"Some place to fuck!" Allen said.

"We are not," not-Emma said. Something about her, something around the eyes, something around her lips, looked familiar, but I was too drunk to map the geography of her face.

"We've got a little surprise for you," Allen said.

I felt the fingers on my knee, breast on my elbow, leg against leg. The pickup truck was too warm, but I didn't know it yet. After the wind, it felt pretty good.

CHAPTER ONE

We took an exit off the highway, and then we turned onto an access road, and then we turned onto a road running through a field.

The woman next to Allen told him when to turn. When the road became gravel, she said, "Not much farther."

We came up on an old white farmhouse. One of the walls had been stripped of clapboards and was covered with Tyvek. Three cars and a pickup truck with a Confederate flag bumper sticker were parked outside.

"They've got the best shit here," the woman next to Allen said. "Just say Sierra sent you, and they'll know what to give you."

"What about money?" I said.

"You don't need money," Allen said. "It's all set."

I opened the door, and then I turned back and kissed Emma on the cheek.

"Hey," she said, but she slapped my ass as I got up.

I slammed the door behind me and stretched a little. The muscles in my shoulder felt all pingy.

When I went up to the porch, I could hear people inside, a radio playing. I knocked on the door, and someone yelled, "Coming, darling."

There was no screen, so when the door opened, she was right there, my KKKer with the still-bloody forehead.

"Come on in," she said.

That's when Allen gunned the engine. His pickup truck ripped it on out of there.

"I think the lady said to fucking come in," a male voice said.

Maybe I could have run toward the fields. Maybe I should have.

CHAPTER ONE

I'm not going to write about it.

"He's just a child," one of them said, and another one flicked on the Bic, tried to stop the flame with my flesh.

It's one of those things I survived.

I have burn marks all the way up my arm, all the way down my leg, and when I kicked out the bathroom window, I had to walk ten miles down to the highway. I had to hide in drainage ditches when their truck went past. The thigh of my jeans was glued to my flesh with pus.

I think they just decided to let me go. They got bored with all of the screaming.

CHAPTER ONE

If you lived through this shit, would you want your misery to go on and on, without a break, in perfect detail, in exact chronological order?

In most stories like this, the callow and rough-edged protagonist decides he doesn't have the stomach for it. He doesn't want to commit acts of violence anymore. He washes the dirt from his hands, cleans his fingernails with a toothpick.

I still want to commit acts of violence.

I usually don't anymore, but I still want to.

You wouldn't want me to touch you with these hands.

CHAPTER ONE

When I got back to Lawrence, everyone knew what Allen had done.

He had given me up for two hundred bucks. Some said three hundred. Sierra was the KKKer's sister.

I have a long brown scar on my left arm and a blotchy pink-brown one on my right thigh.

I'm not going to let you touch these ones.

They're not exactly pretty shapes. I can't just type them out for you.

CHAPTER ONE

For a short time, I slept on the street and I begged for change on Mass.

I had nowhere else to go, so I went back to the skins' house.

"You all right, dude?" Karl, one of the other skins, asked.

"I'm all right," I said, "but Allen's dead."

Allen owned that house. He literally owned it, and I went back and threatened to kill him.

"Shut up," Karl said. "He will kill you, and he'll kill you again. He will break your motherfucking back."

"I don't care," I said, and I went upstairs to sleep on the mattress I sometimes slept on, bowed and hollowed out from so many other bodies.

CHAPTER ONE

I was asleep at the skins' house. Everyone knew what house it was, on account of the parties, on account that it was a bad idea to ask us to turn the stereo down—and I guess Allen knew I was there.

I could hear him from upstairs.

"I never noticed before," he said, "but she's right: he is a chink. He's a stupid chink motherfucker."

He knew I was upstairs. He wanted me to hear.

When I walked down the stairs, I heard Allen say, "That chink is a funny motherfucker." And then he told the story of what happened in Kansas City.

I listened to the whole chinking story, and he didn't tell it half bad. When I shoved my head in the living room, he was talking to a couple of dudes I didn't know, some chick too. The guys weren't skins. They weren't anything. The girl looked about twenty. When she turned to look at me, I saw the thin bones of a smile, her clavicle pushing up through the skin. Her hair was that kind of dyed black that parodies blackness. At some point, I realized it was Allen's sister, Saskia. I had met her just once before.

"So now I'm a motherfucking chink?" I yelled.

"You've always been a motherfucking chink," Allen said.

I flipped him off, and I kind of freaked out, and I kicked the moaning television set right off the stand, and it spit out a couple of sparks and smoked a little bit. Then I dove for Allen, and he kicked me in the side of the head. The two dudes grabbed me. I tried to knee somebody or spit on somebody or bleed on them. I didn't know the two other guys. They were guys in a way that didn't matter. They had their fingers gripped around my arms and my body. They were hugging me in a way. Saskia just watched. She watched everything. Everyone wanted to impress her.

"Fuck you, Allen," I said, and I tried to kick him in the face, but he was too far away. The guys dug into my shirt and skin, tried to smash my feet into the floorboards. Saskia's eyes burnt on and on.

Allen slapped me three times across the face, counting each blow out loud.

"You stupid chink motherfucker," he said. He didn't even seem high. I looked at his bulbous fat-baby head; I had shaved it for him before. He gave me a crazy half smile, and then he kicked me as hard as he could, right in the nuts. A note of blue pain pealed in my testicles, then up through my abdomen. I puked a little bit, and I tried to squirt it on one of the guys holding my arms.

"You always were a fucking pussy," Allen said.

He acted like he was going to kick me again and then laughed. They just kind of threw me down on the floor.

"You want to piss on him or anything, Saskia?" Allen asked.

"Asshole," I said.

One of the other guys kicked me hard in the thigh, then the neck. I was drinking and drowning in thick black sweat and blood. My self couldn't find oxygen. I had a self in there somewhere. I gulped for air that didn't seem to exist anymore.

"Shut the fuck up," the guy said, and then he kicked me again. "Let's kill him."

Saskia didn't say anything at all. Just walked over and stood right over my face. I could see up her skirt to a line of orange panty, a curve of ass. She just stood like that over me, squatted over my face. She tugged her underwear to the side with two fingers, and I could see the pink folds of her labia frowning down, a fringe of pubic hair. Some soft, bare part of her bumped against my nose.

"Don't look," she said in a low, quiet voice. "I can't do it with all of you standing there," she said, louder. "I'll meet you out at the car."

"I'm not leaving you with this asshole," Allen said.

Someone kicked me in the side again, and I felt something creak in my ribs. A hot wave of bruise washed up in my head.

"Hey," she said.

"Sorry," someone mumbled.

She said, "This fuckhead wouldn't dare do shit to me."

I stared up and into her. She smelled like grass and soap.

"Just fucking go," she said. I could hear their dull footstep clomps and then the door thud behind them. I stared at her vulva, squinted, stared some more.

"Get a good look," she said.

We waited for the liquid hiss of it, the strange relief to arrive.

"I'm sort of tempted to do it," she said. She helped me roll out of the way, and then I listened as she pissed a puddle onto the skins' living room floor.

She didn't even look at me.

"I'm pretty sure you owe me one," she said.

Pain floated all around me. I heard it walking around. I heard it slink out the door. She didn't even say goodbye.

CHAPTER ONE

Although you might think I am incredibly fucked in the head, I would have forgiven Allen if he hadn't beaten the crap out of me. I would have continued to shave his head for him with tender and precise care. I wouldn't have stirred any blood to the surface.

I guess I should tell you something else. I am a chink, at least a little bit. You can barely see it in the angle of my eyes. You have to look for the mongrel geometry of it. It's this sliver of a percentage of me, my chinkness.

My father was half Chinese and half English, and my mother was Polish and Mexican and Native American. Both of my parents remain absolutely silent on the mathematics of all this. They killed themselves when I was two days old, and I suppose you should have known about that earlier too.

Allen could have chosen any of these other words: *Polack, spic, Tonto, limey.*

My ancestors fucked in the out of doors. They fucked in the beds someone else actually slept in. I bet your ancestors did this too.

My skin looks slightly browned, like the crust of roasted meat. You wouldn't think I was anything identifiable at all. Just a tan-looking guy with an eagle-beak nose, eyes that lean a bit, and brown hair the color of brown hair. Most people can't even guess at what I might be.

The word *chink* in itself sounds ugly, harsh, like a pencil in an eardrum. You can stuff that word in some kind of hole.

My face is the color of toast. Most of the skins were Anglo-Saxons the color of Elmer's glue.

We were supposed to be above all that shit.

Mainly I'm one of those people who never has enough money.

If you're hung up on race and ethnicity, then fuck you.

CHAPTER ONE

I was pretty beat up, even for me, and beat up was my usual state of being.

I puked a little next to the puddle of piss, and then I thought I needed to call someone, and the only one I could think of was the weird old lady, the English professor I had met a couple of months earlier.

I called her on my cell—not the one I have now, a different one. Marilynne picked me up that night.

"What happened?"

"Shit happened," I said.

Even when I was a small child, the size of a bundled sleeping bag, I could take a punch, pain, humiliation. Isn't that life's smorgasbord? All you can eat?

"You knew they were hyenas," Marilynne said.

"I'm a hyena," I said. "I laugh at all of this shit."

"You do not," she said. On this night, she acted more lucid than normal. Maybe she liked the contrast of someone else's life going awry. She bought me four fifteen-pound bags of ice at a convenience store, and she made me chug Advil and water.

One of my testicles was swollen, and I had a sharp pain like a pointed stick scratching into my throat. I sat in Marilynne's bathtub, and she poured ice in and around and on top of my naked body. My skin had bloomed with red and nicotine-stain yellow. I had a fat violet bruise on my chest that I couldn't even remember. The burns were healing, but some of the skin had broken open, weeping.

She wanted me to go to the hospital.

She added more ice, and I sat there and shivered until my teeth chattered. I let myself shrivel down the drain. She left me alone, but she haunted me even then. On the other side of the bathroom door, Marilynne hummed to herself. It sounded like the buzz of static on a radio station that died several miles ago.

The testicle felt almost normal again. I didn't feel that awful. They hadn't even messed with my face much. I put on an old blue bathrobe of Marilynne's. It was frizzy polyester but clean.

"I'll live," I said to her through the door.

"Aren't you going home?" she asked.

"I don't think I really have one."

"The couch's all yours," she said.

I lurked in the bathroom. I didn't want to look at her. I didn't want her to look at me. The bathrobe smelled like her: mint and something just north of must and whiskey and lilac. One of those fuzzy things, like the pelt of a Muppet, covered the toilet seat. I sat down on it.

"You coming out?" she asked.

"Not now," I said.

"Okay, fine."

She was a good lady.

I sat on that toilet and emptied my head of everything. The air bubbled through and didn't bump into a single thought, then bumped into Saskia. I shook her out, pressed my hands and then my forehead against the cool white porcelain of the bathtub. My pain felt woody and wet, chewable, like a toothpick splintered between teeth.

I thought the guy who said "Let's kill him" had really meant it. That made me happy for some reason, and I know it's fucked up, but I wasn't dead. I took almost all they could deliver, and still I was there. I remembered the pink secret of a vulva. I felt something stir above my bruised left nut. I laughed and took six more Advil.

I sneaked down the stairs and poured whiskey in the dark. I smoked cigarettes and drank and chewed ice cubes.

I slept on Marilynne's couch for six weeks, until all the bruises were gone.

CHAPTER ONE

Here are some random facts about ghosts.

Despite all the wonderful things ghosts say on television and in the movies—all that dark and piquant advice—they don't talk at all. Yes, they look washed out. Yes, you can feel their presence, but it's emotional, not tactile.

Fuck if I know if they can walk through walls.

They're sneaky motherfuckers, though.

Maybe they just materialize.

They don't scare you. They make you feel sad as all get-out, like you've been drained of blood and pumped full of tears.

They are not a comfort.

Ghosts fill your mouth with lonesome, and no matter how much you say, you can't get rid of it.

Ghosts wear the clothes they died in. They don't make a sound.

They are really there.

If you talk to them, they will ignore you.

If you try to touch them, they will shrivel.

If those facts don't seem like facts to you, start your own new branch of science, Ghostology or some shit.

These are the facts.

I've woken up to them, and I've seen them at the threshold of sleep, and I've seen them in sunlight, when they look dappled and almost nostalgic, like some old movie playing on an ancient VCR hitched up to one of those TVs that gets three channels if you screw with the antenna.

That nostalgia grabs you by the throat, and then something cuts it, and you have to think, they're dead, they're dead, and they don't smile at you. They only watch.

~~They wait for something you can't give them.~~

They wait some more.

They are patient, jaded motherfuckers.

A ghost mainly stands there and looks mournful. I've seen them, but I know nothing about them.

I have no philosophy of ghosts.

CHAPTER ONE

Here are some random facts about the Ghost Machine.

There's nothing random about it.

In a previous life, it spewed music as a Sony Walkman. It belonged to my father, and somehow it traveled with me—the only artifact that survived from my birth, my abandonment, to now. In foster homes, my clothes disappeared, my shoes, the blanket my mother knitted, but the Walkman was too crappy to steal. No one wanted it.

It feels eerie on your head. The headphones pinch your ears.

The foam padding has hardened, threatens to crumble.

If it reverted to its previous form and became just a Walkman again, I don't own a single cassette.

Maybe my father fucked with that Walkman somehow. I've been told he was a computer scientist. I think he feared the future. I think he wanted to fuck with it too.

Maybe that Indian shaman really knew magic.

Maybe these are not really facts.

CHAPTER ONE

A phone is all voice, all voices.

CHAPTER ONE

I am not the hero of my own life. Saskia saved me at least three times, and I'm not talking about her constant and unconditional blah-blah-blah, which buoyed me in times of great despair and blasted me with artificial tanning rays on days that were actually overcast. I'm talking kickass, take-charge shit.

If you had a Saskia, your life would be measurably better. Maybe you would be able to quantify it, but as you know, I kind of suck at math.

If her name weren't Saskia, I don't know what she'd look like. I don't know what I'd call her.

We acquire the shape of our names.

I could only be Neptune. My parents tried to shape me in some other way, but my ambitions were astronomical. I don't mean large. I mean to the stars.

To the stars through difficulty, motherfuckers.

CHAPTER ONE

Saskia wanted to run tests, experiments. She thought about these things scientifically.

She wanted to make her ghost brother appear. That was her ultimate goal. She made minute adjustments to the volume, and I watched the Marilynne ghost to see if she reacted. The Marilynne ghost did not react at all.

Ghosts are not scientific.

"What about now?" Saskia said.

"She's standing there, just like before."

"And now?"

"Same thing."

Her lips were pursed, eyes narrowed. When she made an adjustment and asked me to check, she made a small notation in a notebook. When she went to the bathroom, I scrutinized the pad. I couldn't decipher any of it, some personal code.

"I don't think this is a science thing," I said.

"Everything's a science thing," she said. "Underneath, we're all cells."

"Even ghosts?"

"Maybe," she said. She made a small adjustment to the volume of the Ghost Machine.

"Nothing," I said, and she made a note.

CHAPTER ONE

She wanted a sample of ghost flesh, a hair from a ghost head. Her interest was both familial and scientific.

When I grabbed at the ghost, I grabbed at nothing. I didn't want to touch it at all, but I did it for Saskia. I did just about everything she asked.

"She's wearing clothing?"

"Yes," I said. "She's wearing what she had on the night she died."

"You were there?" she asked.

"Yeah," I said.

"Interesting."

She said it in a way that pissed me off.

"I was there the night before, and then I found her body in the morning. I saw her ghost first."

Her look was the kind of inscrutable that makes you want to scrutinize.

"What?" I said.

"It's pretty suspicious," she said.

"You think I killed her," I said. "You think I killed Allen too."

"It's plausible."

"Fuck you."

"You don't think a ghost would haunt her murderer?"

"She's not haunting," I said. "She's just there."

"That's haunting. That's the essence of it."

"I didn't do it," I said. "Either of it."

"You don't think you're capable of it?"

If I was going to be honest, I had to peel back all the skin.

"I'm capable of it, and I know it," I said. "I could do it."

She looked at me.

"But I didn't."

She looked at me some more. Her eyes were wide, wide-set. If I tried to describe their shade, you would say, eyes aren't that color. She pushed back a clump of hair so it collected behind her ear: the better to hear me with.

"I didn't do it," I said.

"It?"

"Murder."

"Do you really think I'd be here if I thought you did?"

She took everything in.

She wasn't someone you could lie to. She wasn't someone you could fuck with.

"How good's your BS detector?" I asked.

"Flawless," she said.

CHAPTER ONE

She was getting pissed about the Ghost Machine. She couldn't adjust it in a way that mattered to the ghost.

"Perhaps there's correlation and not causation," she said. "Maybe the ghost affects the machine and not vice versa."

We sat there and drank beer. The bar was still sort of empty back where we were. It was almost good to be alone with her.

"Tell me about my brother," she said.

"I've already told you," I said. "I can't see him. He's not a ghost, or he's not my ghost or something."

"About him, the real him," she said.

We had been trying shit for hours. The room was hot, and I was peeled down to a T-shirt and jeans. I could smell the vanilla scent she wore and something under it too, her bacteria smell.

I reached over and wrapped my fingers around her wrist. She did not pull away, but I could sense her urge to recede. I didn't touch her hand. I wanted some part of her that didn't touch back. I grabbed skin and bones and ligaments and veins, and her pulse insisted that we were alive. It beat up through my index finger.

"He wasn't always an asshole," I said. "When I first met him, he was in that hardcore band. Remember? They were called Nothing."

"They were so bad," she said. "He just yelled."

"I met him at one of their shows. I crashed at his house that night. I just kept crashing."

"How old were you?"

"Fifteen maybe. He let me move in."

"Move in?"

"I was between," I said, and then I had to pause a bit, "situations."

"Situations?"

"Living situations."

"He wasn't always fucked up," she said. "Right? There were times when he was cool."

"He wasn't completely fucked up. You know that."

"Sort of," she said. "It's hard to remember when he wasn't an asshole."

"He wasn't always an asshole."

"What about that day?" she said.

I knew what she meant, but I didn't want to talk about it.

"What day?" I said.

"That day he beat the shit out of you."

I didn't say anything. I scratched the left side of my face, where I could feel the deep groove of a scar.

"Sorry," she said.

"For what?"

"For bringing it up."

"I don't care."

"Yes, you do."

"You kind of saved me that day," I said.

"Kind of?"

"Okay, you did."

"Maybe I saved him."

"For a while," I said.

"I saved both of you," she said. "He would have killed you."

"I don't think so."

"When I went out to the car, when I left you, he was loading a handgun. He was going to go back in there and blow a hole in your head. That's what he said, something like that."

"You talked him out of it."

"That and one of the other guys just drove away, got us out of there. Allen kept messing with his gun in the backseat, saying, 'Turn the fuck around.'"

We sat there for a bit.

"I'm sorry," she said.

"You saved me," I said. "You don't need to be sorry."

"I'm sorry for telling you this."

I couldn't tell if I was sorry or not. I didn't want to talk to her about that shit. She was beautiful. She made my eyes hurt. She made my brain hurt. A ghost loomed beside her.

"We're not going to figure any of this out."

"You're going to take off," she said.

"What?"

"You're trying to take off. I can tell."

"No," I said, "I'm not," but I was. I was angling for the door, and I thought about ditching all of that, Saskia, the ghost, shithole Lawrence. There's a place out under the I-70 overpass on the way into town where the trains slow down, and I knew how to jump one. I'd done it before, just for the sake of doing it. I could take one of those trains as far as it went. When that one stopped, I'd find another.

"I don't believe you," she said.

"I don't think we're going to solve this," I said. "I need to fucking do something."

"Like what?" she asked.

"I don't know," I said, and then I don't know why, but I told her about the dynamite.

CHAPTER ONE

She reminded me of sunshine, of hard drugs, of the hottest fucking curry they make—you have to beg for more heat and promise not to sue—these things you love that also fuck you up.

I wasn't afraid of her exactly, but she was right: I wanted to get out of there.

When she went to the restroom again, I didn't have to think about it.

I zipped the Ghost Machine up into my backpack next to the dynamite. On the way out the door, I gave twenty bucks to Joey for the tab.

I had the type of plan I usually had.

When I was halfway down the block, my phone rang.

If I had taken a minute more, I could have dug into her purse and deleted my number in her phone. Instead, here she was, sneaking through my ear, almost in my brain.

"Hello," I said.

"You asshole," she said. "Bring it back."

"It's mine."

"The ghost is yours," she said, "but the Ghost Machine belongs to me."

"It's mine too."

"You gave it to my brother, and my brother gave it to me. It's my inheritance."

"I don't care."

"You do care. I can tell. You wouldn't have picked up if you didn't."

I was only outside Louise's bar. I hadn't even made it off the block.

"Fuck," I said.

"Fuck what?"

"Everything," I said. "I'm on the way back."

She wasn't exactly smiling, but she wore this sheen of almost-happiness. I could see it from outside the window, and when I came inside, she hugged me. She held on for a long time.

"I knew you'd come back," she said.

Thing is, I almost didn't pick up at all.

This would have been a different book, I think.

CHAPTER ONE

"If we had met in some other life," she said, "I think we could have liked each other."

"Liked?" I asked.

"*Liked*," she said.

If I were going to write a treatise on ghosts, it would be a completely different book. If I were going to write a treatise on the living, this would be it.

CHAPTER ONE

If you have an idea, write it down. That's my philosophy. You might never have another one.

CHAPTER ONE

Okay, when I said I had never read any of Marilynne's work, I lied. I've read a couple of little things she wrote.

But I don't think I actually lied to you, and in fact, you can go back and check because I just did, and I actually said *I haven't ever read any of her books*, which is true, and as you know, the earth can crack open and a plague of grasshoppers can fall from the sky and the ice caps can melt, but I am here for you, I am in your brain, I'm part of you now, and you wouldn't lie to yourself.

I probably should tell you that Marilynne seemed to be writing a book about me. She left part of it out on her coffee table once. I don't think she left it out on purpose, but maybe she did.

She typed everything she wrote with an old manual.

She liked punishing the letters, smashing them down; at least that's what she said.

Here's what she left out, just a couple of opening paragraphs:

Chapter One

Pluto gave himself a name pulled from the stars. He had blood and shit on his hands, but that doesn't matter. Across town, the old woman he took care of played her violin.

Pluto didn't know he'd kill her, but he would. The old woman thought about death with each saw of her bow. She played inelegantly, harshly even. Still it sounded like music.

She changed my name to Pluto—the poor little planet that's not even a full fucking planet anymore, the one that was cast out. Either that or the cartoon dog. The god of the underworld, I guess too, but that's not the first thing you think of.

The name Pluto seemed worse than the idea that she thought I might murder her.

She didn't even play the violin. Her book was all made up, but it still pissed me off.

You don't ever want to end up a character in a book. You get punctuated. It's black, it's inky. You get crushed between pages.

It's probably better than dying.

CHAPTER ONE

They got rid of Pluto, and Neptune was all alone out there.

CHAPTER ONE

Let's begin again.

Imagine if you could. Nothing good or bad would follow you. You could become something new.

I always think I'll be something new, something different, by the time I get to the next page.

Then I get there, and fuck, it's still me. I'm still half drunk at Harbour Lights.

"Tell me everything you know," I said. "All of it."

"That would take forever," Saskia said. "A whole lifetime."

"I think I could do it in one long afternoon."

"I think you know shit you're not even aware of," she said.

"Nope," I said, "I know nothing."

If only you had been there—you could have vouched for me.

Maybe at that point we were completely drunk, on beer, on failure.

Harbour was dotted with drinkers. We were into nighttime now. Another day was gone, and we couldn't solve any equations about ghosts.

We ordered pizza from the place next door. We devoured grease on crust.

"Can we try," she said, "to pretend all of this shit isn't going on, to pretend the world's normal for a minute?"

"The world's not normal."

"I don't even believe in the concept of normal," she said. "I said pretend."

"We can try," I said. "But everything's so fucked up."

She reached over and grabbed my forearm. "Try harder," she said.

She told me some stuff, the kind of shit that cements together a life. She used to own two cats. She was in AA for a while, but now she wasn't. She was getting a bachelor's degree in physics.

She began to explain. She drew with the dew from our glasses. She made our glasses smash into each other.

She gave me the weight of the falling object; she gave me the height of the fall.

"I did this in high school," I said.

"You did not."

She explained trajectories, something about angles.

"What are you going to do with all this shit?"

"Shit?" she said.

"I'm using it as a general replacement for stuff."

She got kind of dreamy. She twirled the pen and brushed back her hair, and she finished some kind of long calculation.

"So?" I said.

"Huh," she said.

"What are you going to do with all this stuff?"

"Rebuild the world."

We all try to rebuild the world.

Unless, of course, we choose the opposite path.

For a long time, I destroyed mine every chance I got.

CHAPTER ONE

"Why'd you save me that time," I said. I just blurted it out.

Saskia reached across the table, adjusted my chin roughly, as if she needed to see me from some new angle. Pursed her lips.

"I didn't think you had anyone else," she said finally.

"But you didn't have to do it like that. You could have done it some other way."

"I needed to get Allen and the others out of there."

She paused. She made her beer mug collide with my beer mug. It looked like she was concentrating on math in her head. Way in the front of Harbour Lights, a couple of guys tossed darts with their opposite hands; I could tell because of their bad form. Someone had picked an old Radiohead song on the jukebox, back from when Radiohead believed in guitars. You probably know the one.

Saskia reached across the table and ran her hand over my head, down my face. "And maybe I wanted you to see me," she said.

"You said to close my eyes."

"But I knew you wouldn't."

"I don't believe you."

"Fine," she said. Her voice was so low, flat, almost lying on the ground. I had to lean in. "I thought it was the only way you'd tolerate it."

"What?"

"I thought it was the only way you'd let me save you," she said. "They're just parts."

"There are parts and then there are parts. We're not talking a shin bone."

"I have a beautiful shin bone," she said. "It goes all the way up to my knee."

I felt a great and unexpected longing to see her shin bone, to trace its length, to test her reflexes: tickle the sole and let the shin do its thing, a sudden uncontrolled kick.

CHAPTER ONE

"Why don't you just turn yourself in to the police?" she said after I told her about Marilynne and the rest of it.

"Because I didn't do anything."

"Maybe you could help them."

I just shrugged.

She closed her eyes and started taking deep breaths.

We sat like that for a long time. She didn't wear much make-up. When you looked at her, it was all her. I watched the breath go in and out.

"I'm not fucking lying," I said.

"I know," she said. "You're the most honest liar I think I know. I can tell."

Something about her face looked either Russian or elfin: the tip of her nose, the peaks of her ears.

"So what's your plan?" she asked.

"Plan?"

"Like a structured course of action."

I took note of the definition, but I didn't say anything.

We seemed to be leaving Harbour Lights.

We walked down to the Replay, and Eddie, working the door, gave me a look, like *you sure as fuck you should be here?* He said all of this with his eyebrows.

I answered with my shoulders.

I pushed some cash toward him to pay the cover, and he said, "This one's on me. It might be your last Replay visit ever. You think I'm going to make you pay for that?"

"What have you heard, Ed?" I asked.

"Calvin's going to squeeze your heart in his fist."

"Come on," I said to Saskia. I reached my hand back toward her, and she grabbed it, didn't let go.

"Thanks, Eddie," I said.

As we pushed through the crowd out on the patio, I could hear the thrum of the bass jigsawing with the guitar inside. Whatever band it was, they were loud.

One of Calvin's anarchists was there. As soon as he saw me, he whipped out his phone.

"I think we've got about five minutes to enjoy the music," I said.

"We'll dance fast," she said.

Inside, a three-piece punk band—three black guys, I heard they were brothers—was ripping the roof off the place. When they were done ripping the roof off, they slammed it down, and then they ripped it off again. I had seen them before. They could do this about every two minutes. The place was stuffed. The whole room tweaked and tilted.

"Forget drinks," Saskia said, and she tugged me into the mosh pit.

"This is a song called—" the lead singer said, but I couldn't hear the rest. Then the drummer slashed out a beat, and the nameless song thundered up. The music punctured the air around us, and I could feel the bass throbbing in my chest. I could feel Saskia's arm around my waist. Whose arm was it? And whose waist? I could feel my scars letting the music in. And then the vocals kicked in. All we had needed were words, and we didn't even know it.

I could feel the music, like water but lighter, drier. It wasn't like water at all. It was like sexual air. It was the buzz of a bee on your skin.

Saskia pushed me into some guy who pushed me back, and then I was a human pinball. I bounced into a dude I knew, who blew hot sour beer stink into my face and yelped with joy.

The band punished their instruments. I bounced horizontally and sometimes vertically, and I smashed into Saskia, into others, back into her. We listened to the song die.

"We better go?" Saskia said through all of her teeth.

"We better go," I said.

I didn't know I was practicing for the violence to come. It wouldn't have a soundtrack later on.

Sorry for the foreshadowing. I try not to do that shit.

CHAPTER ONE

I assume Calvin showed up with a handful of other guys to kick my ass. Maybe we got out of there just in time.

We booked it down Tenth Street and then down New Hampshire, up Ninth, all the way to Pennsylvania. We were pretty sure that no one had followed us. We backtracked to Mass and sneaked across the bridge to the Jayhawker Motel. Saskia put a room on her credit card.

Her fingers were longish and thin, but they were really about the knuckles. I bumped into her a little, and she made a fist, and she brushed the ridges of her knobby fingers over my cheek. She grabbed my face and just sort of looked up into it. She didn't say a thing, and I didn't say a thing, and she just sort of kneaded my face.

"Are you feeling me or are you shaping me?" I asked. "Sculpting or something."

"I don't know," she said. "Both."

"Good luck," I said.

She kept kneading. Her fingers were warm. My skin prickled. Someone was yelling outside, down on the street, but it was far enough away that it sounded like a whisper. I couldn't make out the words.

"You drunk?" I asked.

She shrugged drunkenly.

"You?"

"No," I said, "just plastered."

"What are they yelling?" she asked.

I bumped into her again, and I felt the boney fender of her hip through her skirt. It felt elegant. She kept exploring my face.

"You in there?" she asked.

Marilynne watched all of this. I don't know how long she was standing there, probably forever.

We did everything fast.

We did it, and we did it again, and then we slept the sleep of the drunk and dying.

If I could remember all of the details of that first time, I'd think about them a lot, but I probably wouldn't tell you.

CHAPTER ONE

In the morning, we woke to the wrong kind of weird.

When I tried to kiss her, she turned away, and I got kind of pissed.

"I didn't need a pity fuck," I said.

She and the ghost just sort of looked at me.

"I'm going to pay for this room for a few days," she said. "You can stay here."

"What about you?" I asked.

"I might stay here part of the time too," she said, and I must have given her a look because she added, "I have class, a job. I have a life. I can't just sit around waiting for you to get arrested or killed or whatever."

She looked at me like I was going to do something stupid. But I wasn't going to do something stupid. I was going to do many things stupid.

I listened to my phone messages, all of them, the new and the old. I listened to the Ghost Machine.

Saskia dozed and tossed and turned and sat up and looked at me every once in a while.

Then I got a call from a number I didn't recognize. I answered it anyway.

"Yeah," I said.

"This Neptune?"

"Who is this?"

"Uranus," he said.

It was Tax. Technology let everyone in.

"You asshole," I said, "you killed her."

"Actually, I heard you did," he said. "That's what I hear, and I hear you have some shit of Calvin's."

"Fuck you," I said. "I didn't kill her."

"I'm going to need you to bring me Calvin's stuff—and you know what I mean by stuff. I'm going to need you to meet me somewhere."

"If I had any stuff, why would I bring it to you?"

"Who saw you leaving the dead lady's house? Who saw your pants covered with blood?"

I didn't say anything.

"It can be a public place—semi-public. Tonight, after last call, come to my house. There'll be a little party."

"I'm not going to your house," I said.

"So name someplace."

I told him about a spot out near the river, the Kaw. I told him exactly where it was. I said to meet me at 1 a.m.

"Yeah, yeah," he said, and it seemed like he was writing it down.

"You killed her, didn't you?" I asked.

"So says the murderer," Tax said, and the phone gave a quiet burp of goodbye.

CHAPTER ONE

Saskia asked who it was and what I was doing.

"Why would you go meet someone like that in the woods?"

"Just in case I need to kill him."

"I'm going out there with you," she said.

"Fuck that. I don't want you involved in this."

"I am involved in this."

"Not anymore."

"Stop it," she said.

"What?"

"You're being awful."

But actually I was just being myself.

She poked her index finger into my chest and then ran it over to my sternum and up into my chin, which she tilted a bit.

"I'm awful all the time," I said.

"So am I."

"I'm really good at it."

"I know," she said.

She didn't smile.

We argued for a while, and then she said fuck it and she left to drive home to Kansas City.

"If I come back tomorrow and you're dead, I'm going to be pissed," she said.

It could have been funny, but it wasn't.

CHAPTER ONE

I climbed back into the bed, buried my dying head under the cool pillow, breathed in the scent left by Saskia's hair: honey and alleyway cigarettes and something like thyme, if I knew what thyme smelled like. Maybe it was basil. There were all these damn spices in the world, and just as many poisons. It was all too much. I lay there until the pillow lost its Saskia-ness.

I went back to my apartment, the top floor of a little house over on Missouri. The door was half splintered and hung on one hinge. My clothes were thrown everywhere. The bureau had been kicked in. The couch was upside down. The futon mattress had two long ugly rips carved into it, like a giant X, and the gray batting leaked out. All my books were thrown in the corner, the paperbacks ripped up.

It didn't matter. Those books lived in my head. It was just stuff. You could get stuff anywhere.

I walked down to the liquor store for a bottle of vodka, then returned to the motel and drank and read *Huck Finn*.

The thing about Huck Finn is I don't think he was as innocent as you hear, and by he I also mean it—because Huck is that book.

There's sex hiding in there, and sodomy, and Twain swore his head off, you know, and if you don't think death and freedom have a codependent relationship, you don't know American history, you don't understand the raft or the river.

I think maybe you need to read it again. Use your imagination this time.

Think about what Twain left out, what he had to leave out.

I don't leave anything out.

CHAPTER ONE

I waited for Tax down by the river in a little clearing in the woods.

I had been there before to drink beer and burn things.

I grabbed some logs and some kindling and piled it all up in the fire pit, just a dug-out ditch paved with stones. I wanted light, so I could see his face. I wanted a bonfire.

The backpack was filled with old paperbacks. I ripped out some pages—the copyrights, the acknowledgments—to get the fire going. I wasn't stupid enough to bring the dynamite, or I was stupid enough not to bring it—one or the other.

I had a good blaze going by the time Tax got there.

When he slipped out of the trees into the clearing, he smiled in a fucked-up way. He clapped his big cymbal hands together. Even the parts of him that were usually ruffled had an unruffled sense. He was enjoying this.

He looked at me, and the ghost looked too. He pointed a little snub-nosed handgun at me.

"Dumb shit," he said.

I bit down on my lip so I wouldn't react, but isn't that a type of reaction?

"Dumb shit," he said again, and he shook his head.

"Fuck you," I said.

"You trying to give me more reasons to shoot you?"

"Did you kill her?" I asked.

He looked at me in a way that could have been thoughtful if you didn't know better.

"Naw," he said, "but I think I know who did."

"It wasn't me," I said.

"I saw all the blood on you." He took two steps toward me and said, "Where's Calvin's stuff?"

"Here." I motioned toward the bag,

"Hand it to me."

I lifted the bag slowly, held it out toward him but not close enough for him to reach.

"Open it," he said.

He stepped toward me, but he didn't grab for the bag. Instead, he pressed the hole of the gun right to my forehead. It felt like a cold little mouth.

When I unzipped the backpack, *The Sun Also Rises* fell out, and then *The Death of the Heart*.

"You fuckhead," he said, and he clicked the safety off.

I always knew that books could fuck you up.

If I moved at all, I'd join the freshly dead.

I held my breath. I tried to ignore the itch between my shoulder blades.

Tax didn't care anymore. He wanted me to stop existing. Not even a Ghost Machine could pull me back.

CHAPTER ONE

That's when something that looked like Saskia stepped out of the woods, and I thought, *oh fuck, she's dead.* I thought she was another ghost.

But it was the real her, and she yelled, "I have the dynamite." She waved another backpack in the air.

"Don't move," Tax said. He swung the gun away from me and aimed it at her.

"I have the fucking dynamite," she said, then turned and ran into the woods. I waited for the sound of a bullet, but Tax didn't fire. She wasn't a ghost, not yet.

"Shit," Tax said, and he started to run too, and then I was right behind him. My arms snapped around his chest and my shoulder drilled into his back. Together we hit the ground, and he somehow lost the gun.

"Fuck," he said. He caught himself with his arms, but my weight pushed him down.

"You asshole," I said. I grabbed him and shook him. I crashed the meat of my hand into the meat of his face, and something crunched in his cheek.

"What the fuck, man," he yelped.

My hands were around his neck, and I just kept squeezing.

I only felt a little bad—like I gave someone ten bucks of bad and they gave me three dollars of bad back in change. You could spend that kind of bad in no time.

He struggled to breathe, and I had to remember that he was human.

If I killed him, who would care?

Then it came to me: I'd care. I let go of his neck, and he pulled in a big gasp of air.

The ground smelled like clover. Do you know that smell? It's almost sweet.

"Let the fuck go," Tax said.

He tried to buck me off, and I rammed a knee into his kidneys.

"Knock it off," I said.

Everything settled but his voice, which was ragged.

"What are you gonna do, faggot," he said.

I pushed his face into the clover with one hand and grabbed my phone with the other.

It took me a few seconds to find the right buttons. I hoped Saskia had run far.

"I've got a murderer out by the Kaw," I said.

"What is your address?" the 911 operator asked.

"There's no address," I said. I described where we were. I told her to look for the fire.

"They'll arrest you too," Tax said.

"I know."

That's when some guy started shouting out in the woods. "I found her," he yelled. "We've got her."

Her had to be Saskia.

"I've got you fucked two and a half ways," Tax said. "You think I'd be out here all alone? I know you're used to stupid, but this—"

I rubbed his face hard into the ground. When I let up, he spit, and then he said, "I'm remembering each of these indignities."

Three people stepped into the clearing. One guy held Saskia in a headlock. Another held the backpack. The police would never get there in time. I used Tax's head for leverage and pushed myself up.

Through the muck of darkness, I couldn't see Saskia's eyes. She kept her head down, like our future was written on the dirt.

"Shit," Tax said. "Calvin's only paying me to kill *him*."

Tax looked around, found the gun, pointed it at me.

The other guys, real ugly fuckers, held on to me and Saskia. I didn't recognize them. I couldn't even recognize Saskia really. She wouldn't look at me. The fire crackled behind us. Her backpack with the dynamite was just lying there on the ground now, waiting for something.

We could hear the police sirens.

The shithead holding me relaxed an inch, and I had just enough time to lunge. I kicked the bag of dynamite into the fire pit.

"Shit!" Tax said.

The nylon stink of it started to burn.

We could have blown up in seconds.

Tax and two of the shitheads scrambled for the bag. I turned and high-kicked the guy holding Saskia. My boot made contact with his skull and socket, with the sponge of his eye.

"Go," I said.

I grabbed Saskia's hand, and we ran.

A gunshot clapped behind us. The breeze of a bullet flew by my neck as we crashed through the underbrush.

We could hear police sirens, multiple cars. They had to have driven down the bike path along the river. I pulled Saskia down toward the riverbank.

"Here," I said.

The sirens were all around us.

We ran down the bank, slid through old dead leaves, and just as I thought, *shit, it's the wrong place*, there it was: the weird outcropping of rock that hid the cave entrance.

I had gotten high in that cave at least half a dozen times. That's why I wanted to meet in the river clearing. There was a way to escape.

Saskia and I clambered under the rock and snaked our way into that cave. We pressed together in the dark, listening to the sirens, to the police yelling through a bullhorn.

We heard some things that sounded like arrests.

We heard tramping feet.

We tried not to move. We barely took in air.

Somebody said, "Where the hell are they?"

"Maybe they had a canoe," someone else said.

We waited it out. We listened until the night quieted down. The river lapped on the bank; some kind of wild animal panted.

I tried to breathe up the darkness. Saskia smelled like cave, like sassafras tea, like roots pulled from the dirt. We hid in the cave the whole time.

If that's not some real Tom Sawyer shit, I don't know what the fuck is.

CHAPTER ONE

If that guy I kicked in the eye was in bad shape, well, at least the cops were coming.

He'd probably never, ever been grateful for the cops before. That's how I rewired him. I made him appreciate law and order.

I don't even like violence anymore.

Even then, I didn't take any pleasure in it.

CHAPTER ONE

Saskia and I went back to the motel.

Tax must have gotten arrested. He possessed the dynamite, a handgun that had been fired. I had been shot at but not shot. The preposition changed everything.

Saskia and I sat together in the bathtub, washing off the night. When the water turned black, we let it drain out, then filled it again. We scrubbed away at each other.

The ghost watched our ablutions.

She really did physics. She had all kinds of heavy and obscure textbooks to prove it. She explained to me how it all works, those balls tied to string that knock into each other again and again. All it takes is one ball to start the process. I can't explain it back to you.

She explained the physics of a mosh pit. I listened. I swear.

It was interesting, but you can't memorize your entire life.

CHAPTER ONE

"Why'd Allen do all that to me?" I asked.

"He was fucked up," she said. "You know that."

"Yeah, yeah," I said, "and I fucked the girl that he used to fuck. Blah, blah, blah."

"He knew it was stupid," she said.

When she looked at me, her face seemed eighty percent eyes. She tucked a sheaf of hair behind her ear, then bit the middle fingernail of her left hand.

"Did you kill him?" she asked.

"What? Fuck. No, no," I said.

She stared at me just like the ghost did.

"Did you kill *her*?" she asked.

"No!"

"Maybe I need to turn you in."

"You are just like your brother," I said. "He beat the shit out of me. He let fucking fascists torture me."

"Fuck you," she said.

"He said that to me too." She started crying, but I could tell she was trying to stop. Her shoulders hiccupped a little.

"He was a shit," she said. "He was stupid. He was a sadist. He got high and drunk and pushed people into furniture. You're not the only one he did shit to."

"What?" I said. "What did he do to you?"

I got up close to her, and her face fluttered before mine.

"Not like that," she said.

"What then?"

"Nothing that bad," she said. "He punched me a few times. Once he whipped me with a belt."

Marilynne just stood there, watching, I guess.

I tried to imagine Allen's ghost.

I felt fresh hate. I wanted him to die all over again.

CHAPTER ONE

Mainly I try to tell as much truth as exists in any one moment.

CHAPTER ONE

She had a stripe of old scar on her lower back and I thought, *Allen did this.*

"It's not like I'm broken."

"I know," I said.

"It's all healed over."

"Sort of," I said.

"Can't we just be broken together?" she said. "Can't we just be us?"

She stood up, and that made her all muscle, tight and corded and firm.

She grabbed me by the hips and pulled me toward her. My hand was on her hip. Her lips traced my eyebrow, found my lips. My other hand found her breast. Her hand found my penis. I think that's how it went.

We spent about eight hours in bed. We didn't get much sleep.

I could have stayed in bed with her forever.

I think so anyway. I think there are pills for that.

The shitty, busted-down bed was like a square, fat cloud. It was seeded with lust.

Maybe that's how it could have gone for the rest of time, but isn't it clear to you that stupid shit happens to me? I make it happen.

CHAPTER ONE

"I feel hunger to the second power," Saskia said.

"Meaning?" I asked.

"Meaning my hunger is multiplied by itself."

I dug my fingers into the bark of an orange Saskia had in her purse, then into the flesh. I pulled the whole thing apart. My hangnails tingled, and there were all these sections to separate and de-pith. I offered some to her, and she shook her head.

"It's good," I said. "Like a little citrus earth."

I ate a piece. "Canada," I said.

"Here's South America," I said, and I held it up to her lips.

She said, "Your continental proportions are all wrong."

"I'll rethink," I said. She nipped the piece from my hand. Her teeth looked like delicate cleavers.

"You will not die of scurvy," I said. "Not on my watch."

If Saskia were multiplied by herself, I don't think she would be bigger. I think just the idea of her—her her-ness, her Saskia-ness—would expand.

If I were multiplied by myself, it would be like splitting an atom. I'd explode. My me-ness is already too big, too messy.

If Marilynne were multiplied by herself, she would retreat into her house, fear everything, lean on me for stuff, stab her hand with glass, die in a horrible way.

If you were multiplied by yourself, well, I have no fucking idea. Maybe you'd need several copies of this book.

CHAPTER ONE

Saskia was not a placebo.

Saskia did something to my body temperature, to the receptors in my brain. She broke down all of my muscles. She could make my legs give out. If I could explain these things to you—if I had those capabilities—I probably wouldn't.

If you want someone who explains, go read some other book.

I'm not just talking about sex, although when I was pressed up and into her, I felt more alive than at almost any other time in my life. It was the same sensation as being in great pain. Isn't that when we're most human?

I know, I know. It's fucked up.

Saskia slipped under the covers next to me, nestled into me. She smelled like fire, which I am differentiating from the smell of smoke. She wasn't smoky. She smelled like fire and something citric, like grapefruit.

"I like your smells," I said.

She rubbed her hand over my stomach and then lower. "I see."

She kept me wrapped in her hand. I breathed her in.

"What are we doing?" she asked.

"Resting," I said.

"I'm asking a larger question."

I had never been good at things like that. You shouldn't be all surprised.

We didn't have any rules. We didn't have to talk about it. It was obvious neither one of us wanted the wrong kind of pain.

"Harder," she said.

"Harder?"

"Faster."

I strove for velocity. It was something about physics.

"You get on top," I said, and we tried to roll together, to stay attached. She had to climb back on, to remount. I looked up at her face, set, solemn. She went fast and then faster.

Velocity like that doesn't last.

CHAPTER ONE

"Allen always said to stay away from you," I said.

"And?" she said.

"The implication was he'd break your fucking back, seriously wreck you, if you got involved with his beloved sister."

"I don't think that's what he meant," she said. "I can fuck up guys pretty much all by myself."

"Meaning?"

"If I love you, I love you at ninety-five miles per hour," she said.

"I don't think that's what he meant."

"I try not to waste my time worrying about messages from the dead," she said.

But that wasn't true. I think that's the only time she lied to me. The only time, plus two others.

CHAPTER ONE

Then, of course—there's always a *then*, and always an *of course*. Then, of course, I fucked it up.

"He did this, right?" I couldn't see it, but I smoothed the small of her back, near the scar.

"Don't touch it," she said.

"It still hurts?"

"No," she said, "I just don't like having it touched."

"He did it."

"Yeah," she said.

"When?"

"I don't really know."

We were wrapped up together. My leg was in between hers. Her arm was wrapped around my waist. We breathed into each other's mouths.

I knew she was lying, and I knew then when he had done it. She knew I knew.

She didn't move or say anything. I waited.

"I'd do it all again," she said quietly.

Then she disentangled herself. Then she started putting on her clothes.

"I'm getting out of here," she said. "This is too fucking much. I didn't think it was, but it is. I'm freaking out."

"Oh," I said.

"I'm sorry," she said.

"It's fine," I said.

"You can have the Ghost Machine."

"Whatever," I said.

"I'm sorry," she said.

I wasn't really looking at her. She came up and touched my shoulder, and I shrugged her away.

"Are you trying to make this worse? Rub it the fuck in?"

"Don't get mad," she said. "It's just too much."

"Fuck you," I said.

"I'm sorry," she said, and her voice wasn't her voice.

I might have sat down. I could hear her rummaging around.

"What are you going to do?" she asked.

"Whatever the fuck I want," I said.

"I'm serious!"

"Just get the fuck out of here."

"Don't say it like that," she said. "I feel awful."

I looked at her then. I figured it was the last time. She was embarrassed, angry, and her eyes were wide and tearing up. I had fucked up something beautiful.

"You don't even look like you," I said.

I reached out a hand toward her, and she didn't take it. I let my arm hang there.

"This is not a big fucking deal," I said. "Just forget it. Fucking go."

I closed my eyes. I heard her creaking over the floorboards. I heard the zipper of something opening, displaying its guts, closing. I heard the door. I heard her whisper goodbye.

CHAPTER ONE

I forgot one thing.

Before she left, she said, "I only gave them four sticks of dynamite." She handed me a backpack with the other two.

She left me the Ghost Machine and two sticks of dynamite.

For a while after that, I didn't give a shit about anything.

I mean I gave even less of a shit than normal.

If Calvin killed me, okay, whatever, and if a ghost hovered by my side, no biggie, and if I got arrested and charged with murder, sure, fine—I'd survived worse.

I went to the bars.

With my hood flipped up, I could have looked like almost anyone at all.

Why didn't the cops just come and arrest me? I wasn't hard to find. Maybe I'll ask them later. Maybe they just thought it would be a better book.

At that point, I thought Tax did it. He ran the wrong way in the woods, and they arrested him with four sticks of dynamite and a snub-nosed handgun, and I thought he'd be charged with Marilynne's murder.

I believed in a lot of stupid things, but you know that already.

Maybe it seems like I was in denial, and no, I'm not denying it.

I went to the bars, and the ghost went with me. The dynamite too.

When in doubt, I had a drink. I was always in doubt.

If I didn't tell you this earlier, I should have. Maybe this should have come first.

CHAPTER ONE

Maybe the dead think no thoughts.

Marilynne is dead, and the brown crinkling leaves are dead, and the doornails are dead, and the dead hate us for our carbon dioxide, our mouthwash, our American cheese served on burlap crackers. When you're dead, you'll miss these things. I miss them already, and I'm only lying here in the dark, writing. If these words don't make sense, don't blame me. Blame the dark.

It might help if you read this in the dark too.

We can be simpatico. Shut off the lights and see if we get along.

CHAPTER ONE

Throughout this whole thing, sometimes I almost forgot about Marilynne, and sometimes I didn't do anything at all. I sat down and read *Huck Finn* a lot, but only during the boring parts. I recommend it to you too: you may read a book during the boring parts.

Out on the Replay patio, the ghost slouched and hovered. Not literally—her feet seemed to touch the ground. If they're with you long enough, ghosts become commonplace, the way you grow used to a tumor, a smoker's cough. I barely noticed her. I was inured, perhaps immune, to ghosts. If she had a purpose, it was lost on me.

I had bought two drinks at the bar, and I lined them up next to each other. A fly seemed to be dying in one. One of the drinks tasted more like gin, and the other tasted more like tonic. Neither tasted like dead fly. I drank from one and then the other, and my tongue began to feel junipery and light.

I read until my drinks were gone. I crushed the ice with my frozen teeth. I juiced every molecule of alcohol out of my glass. All the late-night people had awoken, and some had come outside. I could see tattoos that said BLACK FLAG and rolled-up jean cuffs and hair the color of cherry cough drops. I could see lips that wanted to kiss and teeth that wanted to bite and tongues that wanted to waggle until words came out. Every part of every person wanted something.

Everything I did in Lawrence led to this: this moment in the Replay. There were all these moments there.

I read until they yelled last call.

I read until they threw me out on the street.

CHAPTER ONE

At the little blue house on Ohio, I saw some lights on. I didn't knock. I didn't know who really lived there, but I'd been there before.

"What time is it?" I said to a hipster-looking dude with an ironic mustache and a flannel shirt.

"It's got to be something," he said.

"I know," I said, and he handed me a semi-cold can of beer, which I can't quite remember the brand of but I will happily lie about if some major brewery would like to pay me a lot of money to advertise it here. It was really wet. It tasted like beer.

I woke up at the stranger's house, and then I biked out along the Kaw River, sweated through two layers of shirt, punished my stolen bike, tried to let the toxins seep away. I pushed way out of town, past the interstate, past the fields past the interstate.

My head was gone, and a bulb of hurt had taken its place. It throbbed and burned. I felt kind of lonely and ready to try again. The horizon was a vast grimace.

In my head, I kept walking into her house, and Marilynne kept lying on the floor, face down, like some sort of collapsed prayer toward the earth, and I kept thinking she was joking, and I kept saying, "Come on, get up, get up."

And then I felt sweaty and rough, and my pulse split my head into two parts, dead and alive, and I yelled, "Get up, get up, get the fuck up."

When I flipped her over, one eye was open, the other cob-webbed with pink. The left cheek was smashed in.

In my head, I kept touching Saskia, and then we kept yelling at each other.

I try again. You have to give me that.

When I fuck things up in my head, I try again.

CHAPTER ONE

Have you forgotten where you were?
Me too.

CHAPTER ONE

I'll bet you thought I'd never get back to being at Jimmyhead's house. But we're back. It seemed like the safest place for me to sleep away an afternoon. I had to break a window to get in.

He found me on his couch, *Huck Finn* steepled over my chest.

"What the fuck are you doing with my copy of *Huck Finn*?"

"I'll buy you a new one," I said.

"I almost called the cops on you the other day, dude," he said. "I wanted to do it, even though I know you didn't kill her. I'd be able to tell if you had. But I just wanted to get you the fuck out of my house."

He had the tips of his fingers pressed together and he brought them up and pressed them against his lips and his chin. He spoke through that lattice of flesh and bone.

"You have some kind of badass karma," he said.

I just sort of looked at him.

"As soon as it's dark, I'm out of here," I said.

"You owe me three bucks for bologna and like six bucks—no, ten—for that book."

"I broke your window too," I said.

"Asshole," he said, and then he brought us each another beer.

We sat there waiting for something that didn't arrive.

A few minutes later, he said, "I'm just ripped up by all of this."

"I feel like my guts are squished up into my heart," I said.

"Up near your lungs?" he said, and pushed his forearm up toward the top of his chest.

I nodded, and the ghost mooned over it all.

"So what are you going to do?" he asked.

"Maybe just leave town."

"Good call," he said. It was almost dusk. "And if you need anything, don't ask me."

CHAPTER ONE

You've wasted at least, what? Two hours reading this shit? Maybe just thirty minutes if you skimmed. Three hours, maybe more, if you had to stop and Google *Ghost Machine* and *Ad Astra Per Aspera* and *Neptune*.

You'll never get that time back, and now you're fucked. You might not have any happy choices anymore.

If you quit reading, you'll never know what happens, not really, not in the right way, not even if you skip to the end. It won't make any sense. None of this makes any sense, but still.

For a long time, I didn't want to finish this either.

For a long time, I couldn't finish this.

I thought it would never end.

CHAPTER ONE

I felt my life sloshing inside me. I was 32% sadness, 3% college dropout, 2% drunk, 9% hopeless, 8% lust, .5% gin, .5% tonic, 17% ennui, 7% bad beer, 6% hunger, 10% guilt, and 5% unsure of my math.

I thought about just turning myself in. To the cops. To Calvin.

I looked up Massachusetts Street. Downtown Lawrence is really just five and a half blocks of two-story brick buildings—stores and restaurants and bars below, apartments above—big sidewalks for the undergrads to puke on, and once in a while a sickly tree stuck in a big cement pot. Quantrill had burned this town, and the hippies had saved it back in the 1970s with their organic bakeries and their ear-candle shops, and now Starbucks and frat boys thought they owned the place. Three cars whirred by and I breathed in the goopy air of night. I peered at a neon sign. It glowed like blood seeping out of a wound. I believed in the red light, Pabst Blue Ribbon right from the can.

When I saw a cruiser coming, I ducked into the Replay again. I wasn't ready for the cops yet.

CHAPTER ONE

Uncle X was inside at the bar.

He said, "Neppy!"

Uncle X knew all the fringers, the skins, the anarchists. He stayed out of shit, but he knew everyone.

He circled his arm around my neck, pulled me to his rough face. He yelled in my ear, "Some friends of yours are kind of pissed off, you wanker."

"They can fuck themselves," I said.

"Anatomically doubtful," he said.

In his right hand, Uncle X hoisted a pitcher of Guinness, the beautiful black murk of tar and dead brain cells.

"It's full of vit-a-mins," he said, and he poured me a glass. The first mouthful brought peat moss and smoke and burnt toast.

I looked at all the pretty nihilists. A girl with green lips pouted at me, and I pouted back, and we didn't say a word, and then our moment was over. A girl I once knew was bumping her hips into invisible hips adjacent to her. She had blond hair that drooped all the way down her back. She could have tucked it into her jeans, and I once encouraged her to do this, and she never did, and she didn't even wave at me, and a black-haired punk in a Mekons T-shirt gave me the finger. He had a mushed-up stack of hair on his head. It looked so casual that you knew it took effort. He was wired by something. I wanted what he had, and if you looked at him you would have wanted it too. He had the answer to something. You could feel it.

Out of the corner of my eye, I saw someone who looked like Saskia. It looked so much like Saskia that it had to be Saskia. It was kind of fucked up. I was kind of fucked up. She was kind of beautiful. She was across the room by the pinball machines, and I felt a hot burst of blood surge in my head. She looked at me inscrutably, and I shrugged in her direction. She wasn't a ghost, except in the way that she was. This is the only ghost metaphor in the entire book. The other ghosts are real.

"Who are you looking at?" Casey asked. I didn't even know when Casey got there. I didn't even know why she was talking to me.

I shrugged at Casey and shrugged back at Saskia. I was a shrugging machine.

"That girl over there," I said. "Don't look."

"You don't look."

"I wasn't," I said.

Casey said, "I thought you fucking killed her." Her voice sounded like a dry sponge scrubbing against her throat.

Casey had the glint of a knife in her eye, something sharp and shiny; her cornea was dangerous. Saskia was gone now.

"I didn't kill her," I said. "I was with you."

"I can barely even remember that," Casey said.

I said, "I can barely remember anything."

Casey played with her hair, and she played with her eyes, rolling them up and rolling them down; she could go clockwise and counterclockwise. She rolled them so much it signified nothing. That was one of the things I used to like the most about her.

Then I was looking at my little phone. She was looking at her little phone too. It was some kind of ending.

The non-ghost Saskia was definitely gone too.

CHAPTER ONE

"I am one drink away from just being morose," I said.

"Isn't it pretty to think so," Missy the bartender said.

I could feel it: a beautiful fuzzy hum in my mouth, in my brain, in my veins. Some of us were meant to throw our heads back and pour the stuff down our throat. Marilynne was like that. She knew how the stuff worked: the gin, the words, the smell of a pencil, the white page waiting for you to fuck it up with all kinds of scratching that might be wisdom or, more likely, just evidence that you're alive.

My cell phone rang, and I answered it quick. I could barely hear over the crowd, the jukebox. I had to shout.

"Who is it?" I asked.

"Me," a female voice said, and I knew, but I pretended I didn't.

"Me?"

"Saskia."

"And," I said.

"And what?"

"Why are you doing this?" I said. "What do you want?"

"To save you," she said.

I didn't say anything.

Maybe I didn't want to get saved. Maybe I didn't need to be saved. Maybe I didn't deserve to be saved. Maybe she was a liar.

"I'm still fucked up about this," she said.

"I am too," I said, and then I hung up.

CHAPTER ONE

I could feel last night's beer fizzing away in my skull. It joined the beer from the night before and maybe the night before that. It felt like battery acid cut with Clorox and ammonia. I could feel my brain cells dying. Each one hollered, convulsed, and then took its own life.

I had slept in my trashed apartment. The door wouldn't even close fully. The ripped-up mattress gnawed on me like a giant mouth.

Another brain cell committed some kind of shuddering death, and my whole body trembled.

If enough of them died, I could just sit in the corner and drool, smell my armpits, whimper.

Sunlight suffused the apartment, like liquid pain being poured in my eyes. Each thought seemed to require brain surgery.

I pulled on last night's pants, which were marinated with last night's smoke. I selected a T-shirt that looked wrinkled enough to hide the dirt. My hair was smooshed down with pillow breath. I shuffled down the stairs, through the streets.

I retreated to The Bourgeois Pig.

People were stirring their coffees too loudly, but it was dark in the back, and I slopped some coffee into my mouth. It tasted like an earthy, happy punch in the guts. I could feel the caffeine buttering up my veins. I would probably live.

CHAPTER ONE

I pulled out the Ghost Machine and listened a bit. It always played something new, some moment stolen from my life.

The machine clunked, whirred.

"This here's Neptune." I knew Allen's voice right away. He was talking to a group. I could hear the background sound of people. I remembered: it was when he introduced me to some of the other skins. It was almost an initiation.

"He's a chickenshit," someone shouted.

"Stuart," Allen said, "I will kick your ass right now."

"Sorry," Stuart said.

"Sorry what?" Allen said.

"Sorry, Neptune."

"Neptune's one of us now," Allen said. "His blood is our blood. When we bleed, he bleeds too. When he bleeds, we bleed with him."

There was the sound of a beer can spritzing open. I remembered Allen pouring it over my shaved head. I listened to the sound of baptism.

Another click, another whir.

I recognized my voice even as it seemed estranged from my existence, from my belief in my voice. It wasn't higher or lower, just different, but I could tell I was younger.

This is what it said.

"My great hope—well, not great—but my hope remains for some sort of freedom." And then someone laughed, not me, and then a girl's voice said, "Keep going," and I said, "You can't put it into words. When you put it into words, it falls apart."

I was fourteen, I think. We weren't drunk, but we weren't sober. I had run away from a foster home. I was giving a manifesto in some girl's bedroom out in Johnson County, the fancy suburbs south of Kansas City. I didn't even know her, really. She demanded manifestos, and I slept on the floor next to her bed. The next morning her parents called the cops.

That girl made you tell her what you believed. She had bed sheets printed with cartoon ponies.

"Say it," she said. "Say what you believe."

Then the machine clunked again, whirred again.

"Marilynne," I said, "I'm here with Kurt Cobain."

I was talking to her on the phone about this guy I met in San Francisco. He looked like Kurt Cobain. He even sang like him, but an old version of Kurt, one who had never died. The guy worked hard to do all this pretending. It got him free drinks. It got him drugs. It got him laid.

"Who?" she said.

"Kurt Cobain."

"Don't know him," Marilynne said. "Where are you? Could you run down to Dillon's? I need a gallon of ice cream and some tonic water."

"I'm in San Francisco."

"What time is it there?" she asked.

"I don't know," I said, and then I must have looked down at my phone. "It's 2:38 a.m. What time is it there?"

She said, "So you think of me when you're in San Francisco?"

"I thought you'd want to know about Kurt. I figured I should call."

That's what I said, but I think I just wanted to hear her voice. I missed her.

"What happened to him?" she said, and she sounded like she was inches away from me. She sounded like she was bleeding gin.

"He didn't die," I said. "Everyone thinks he died, but everyone's wrong."

"Good for everyone. What about my tonic water?"

Then fake Kurt shouted to me, "Let's go smoke something."

"I've got to go," I said into the phone, and out of the phone, I yelled, "Wait up."

"Don't go," Marilynne said.

And then I must have pressed a little rubbery button on my phone and killed her voice.

I don't know what she said in Lawrence, Kansas. Her voice was gone. In San Francisco, fake Kurt said to me, "Your mom sounds like a bitch."

The Ghost Machine clunked, then whirred.

"I just wrote that we're hanging out," I said.

"Is that what we're doing?" a female voice said. It sounded like Saskia.

"I'm finishing a book," I said.

It pissed me off. Now the fucking Ghost Machine was making shit up. I couldn't remember this conversation at all. I had only read one book in front of her, and I didn't even finish it. I never said that shit to her.

That's what I thought anyway. That's what I guessed. Or maybe it was playing my whole life now, not just the past. Maybe it was the future. Maybe I would have this conversation with her someday. Maybe she'd come back.

Or maybe I could just plug myself into this machine and hear it all, pretend it happened, live a virtual life. I could surrender to the machine, believe everything I heard, sit in a coffee shop and let it fuck with my brain.

The machine clunked again, whirred again.

"You little shit," someone said, and I heard the sound of flesh on flesh.

The machine clunked again, whirred again.

"Neptune Asshole," a voice said, "like we're brothers."

The machine clunked again, whirred again.

"I love you," Marilynne said.

The machine clunked again, whirred again.

I heard punching and breathing.

"Stop," I said. It sort of wheezed out of me.

Someone was breathing heavily. I heard myself groan. The punches didn't stop.

I wasn't throwing them. I didn't want to think about it.

The machine clunked again, whirred again.

I heard the hiss of a lighter.

I heard myself screaming.

Then the cassette spokes whirled without catching for a while. No sound came out, and it pissed me off, and I slammed my hand down on the table next to the machine. It clunked. It whirred.

"Maybe we can't do it—because of the baby," a woman said. I didn't recognize her voice.

"We should bring the baby in too. Our baby shouldn't suffer through life either," a man said.

"No," the woman said. "Please don't do it to the baby." She began to cry.

"We talked about this," the man said.

The woman didn't say anything.

"Fine. Put him outside. Someone will find him, one of the neighbors."

I heard shuffling.

"Hand me that blanket," the woman said.

"Hurry up," the man said.

I heard a door open and then close.

Someone—the woman—hummed. It wasn't a lullaby. The baby cried and then hushed and then cried again.

"We love you," the woman said. "You are loved." She was sobbing. "You are loved."

I heard lips on baby skin. The crying stopped.

For a few seconds, the tape played the sound of nothing.

Then a door closed quietly.

Baby Neptune cried and cried. It went on for a long, long time.

CHAPTER ONE

I had the backpack with two sticks of dynamite. I put the Ghost Machine in next to them.

I bought a collapsible shovel at the camping store. It cost me two pitchers' worth of beer.

On my stolen mountain bike, I rode down Massachusetts. A hippie at Free State waved to me. A police cruiser drove by going the other way, then turned around, hit the lights and the siren.

It felt like the end.

I pedaled with my knees up by my ears. I was bent over, aerodynamic, committed to the angle of escape.

At the red light at Mass and Sixth, I raced on through. I whooshed toward the bridge.

I pedaled harder, and the lights flashed right behind me. Then something miraculous happened. The cop car blew past me and pulled over a Subaru full of college kids. Jam band stickers glared at me from the bumper.

I thank those kids for their traffic violation. I appreciate their temporary pain, their eighty-buck fine, which bought my deliverance. I'm sorry they like jam bands. I can't do anything about that.

Maybe it's hubris that makes me believe all cops are looking for me, but I prefer to think of it as a healthy defense mechanism.

As I slipped over the bridge and down to the trail, the bike felt lighter. Seeing cops accost someone else turns you into something airy and bright. It's the feelings the stars look like, but not what they are.

CHAPTER ONE

If I had to destroy, I would destroy only grass, a backpack, a Ghost Machine.

If you had a Ghost Machine, you'd try to destroy it too.

I went to work. I began to dig. I won't tell you about the digging.

My goal is to bore neither you nor me, but I think I'm bored now.

Let's turn the page.

Let's blow something up.

CHAPTER ONE

I shoveled till my hands ripped up, then I shoveled some more. The hole was the shape of a grave, but I didn't realize that until it was already done. I put the Ghost Machine in there, and then I put in the backpack. I had some rolled-up paper, which I lit with a lighter, and when I tossed it in the grave, I ran like a motherfucker.

It made a firecracker sound multiplied by war, and a gout of fire shot out of the hole and then died on itself. When I went back to stamp out some sparks in the grass, the shovel had melted beyond use. A sign: you, Neptune, are not a gravedigger. Another sign: the shovel was swirled into a comma.

The Ghost Machine and the backpack and the dynamite were gone, incinerated.

My ears rang as I poked around in the ashes of the grave, and then I thought, *oh, fuck, oh, holy and lost fuck*, because Marilynne's ghost stared down at me from the edge of the earth. I thought killing the Ghost Machine would make her disappear. I guess I thought she'd die again, but I didn't think of it as murder. I thought of it as release.

You can't blow up a ghost. You can't blow up a memory. You can black it out for a while, sure, but just for a while. It's like those computers. Even when you think you've trashed all your data, it's still living on somewhere in the digital gloom.

I had destroyed as little as possible with a great amount of force.

My ears rang. Specks of light salted my vision.

To the stars through difficulties, motherfuckers.

CHAPTER ONE

I was and am so sick of ghosts.

Ghosts are pathetic, passive. They just stand there.

If you think squirrels are dumb, wait until you see a squirrel ghost: it's dumb to the second power.

Don't get like that. I can make math references. Just don't expect me to solve the actual equation.

I'm pretty sure the second power means you multiply one thing by itself.

My own ghost would have the same intellectual deficits. That's a given.

My ghost would have to ask someone about that second-power business just to be sure.

My ghost might just stare at you dumbly. I'm already good at that.

Marilynne's ghost almost never moved. Her face was bashed in on one side. If you knew she was hit by an iron, you could make out the shape of it. I didn't like knowing. Sometimes the ghost wore the oven mitt, sometimes it didn't.

I thought maybe ghosts got confused. Maybe they lost things. Maybe they tried to send signals.

If you see a ghost, don't bother looking for signals. I've already warned you about looking for clues, though I know you don't listen. Ghosts aren't here to tell us something.

If you're looking for messages, you're better off reading a book.

CHAPTER ONE

Fuck that. Books don't have messages either. Just read.

It's just a story. Everything happened, but it's just a story. So is your life. It will end at some point. When in doubt, love someone until you're weak and feverish and bent at some new angle.

And congratulations by the way: that's your first step in becoming a master of origami.

CHAPTER ONE

I walked over to the bike and headed back. As I rode toward town, another cop car drove toward me.

The police must have received a call about the explosion.

I had to scoot off the bike path because the car took it all up.

The cop driving rolled down his window. I didn't recognize him.

"You hear anything out here?" he said.

"Like what?" I said.

"Huge fucking explosion?"

"Nah," I said.

CHAPTER ONE

You need to understand that as you read this I am doing complex fucking things to your brain chemistry. Well, not me, this book, but as we've already discussed, I both am and am not—amn't—this book.

I don't care if *amn't* isn't a word.

As you read this, you will become more empathetic. Scientists—or at least psychologists—have confirmed that the act of reading helps you care more for others, to understand, to sympathize with their plight. After you read this, you will reach outside of yourself. You might pet a slightly mangy dog. We can't be sure of the results. It's up to you to put it into action.

But I've done the hard work already. Your brain chemistry is changing. If we shove you into an MRI machine right now, who knows what parts of your brain will pulse with light?

I know actually. The good parts.

And if we ever get to the end, I promise some shit:

You will feel new somehow. You will have gone on a journey. You will embrace new words.

I'm just joking about that.

We'll never get to the end.

And I promise you nothing.

CHAPTER ONE

Of course you think it's stupid that I kept going to the same places, places where I was recognized, places where people knew Calvin, places where I drank my brain into agitated stillness. But where else would I go?

These were my places. These were my people. The Replay was the closest thing I had to a real home. You know what Robert Frost said about that shit.

And it's not like I had a car, a house, parents. What if I took all of those things away from you? Where would you go then?

My life kept on ending up, and after every end, I found myself at the Replay.

I thought I had blown away the sun, but outside the bar, it was somehow still afternoon. A child with a streak of dirt on his face, mittened and stocking-capped, shook a Styrofoam cup at me. A couple of coins clanked. It made a lonely sound.

My face had to be dirtier than his.

His jacket looked brand new, same with his jeans. He was probably seven. The cup was clearly unused, perfect in its foam awfulness, no coffee drips.

The child eyed me from under his bangs. It wasn't cold enough for mittens. He booped something into a cell phone— I could see his pointer finger extended and pushing out of the general mitten area, the international symbol for "I want you to believe I have a gun." He turned his fake gun back into a hand and then slipped the phone away.

"Hey, kid," I said.

He chanted a little songlike thing: "Spare change, spare change, you've got to chain-ain-ange, spare change."

"I don't think you really need to be out here," I said.

"Are you calling me a poseur?" he asked.

"Yup."

When he winked, he used everything above his neck, like he couldn't get the eyelid to blip up and down without rocking his head.

"You Neptune?"

"Who's asking?"

"I've got a message for you," he said.

He had a round face, sort of squat and wily. I knew he had brushed on the dirt himself. I should have thought of this child as a threat, but instead I thought of him as a child. I believe mothers and fathers make this same mistake.

"A message?" I said. "From who?"

"From whom," he said.

He did his whole-head wink again.

"I'll make a grammar note," I said. I winked back at him, with a full head bob and an upper-torso bend.

He winked too. I felt like we could keep on doing this for the entire afternoon, wink for wink, a frisson of aerobic activity.

I thought about my pronouns.

"Who is sending me the message?" I asked.

"It's on the way," he said, and then a car screeched down Tenth, slammed into a parking space, and Calvin and two of his boys jumped out.

"Shit," I said.

"Asshole," the child said.

I turned to book it, but the kid threw himself at me, grabbed my legs. I'd nearly kicked him off when Calvin grabbed me from behind.

"Fuck you, Calvin," I said.

"Don't swear in front of him," Calvin said.

"Just like you said," the kid said. "He's a real piece of work."

"Who is that little shit?" I asked.

"That's my boy," Calvin said.

Calvin had his arms wrapped around me, while the other two guys took up position on either side of me.

"It's too bad about your leg," Calvin said.

"What?" I said, and then the guy on my right drove his combat boot into my right shin.

"Fuck," I said and then added several more fucks.

"Help him in the car, boys," Calvin said.

They wrapped their arms around my shoulders like I was limping off a soccer field. The one on the left smelled like weed and talcum powder.

"Fuck you guys," I said.

"Not in front of the kid," Calvin said.

CHAPTER ONE

So Calvin had me. He was driving, and I could see his big eyes staring at me via the rearview. His pores looked huge. I was wedged in between the two other dudes in the back of the car.

"I never thought I'd see your motherfucking face here under the circumstances," Calvin said, "but then I thought, who the fuck's dumb enough to go out to the Replay when he's wanted for murder? There's only one answer to that question."

Calvin glared via the mirror.

"Where's the dynamite?" he asked.

"I blew it up," I said.

"I think we have to kill him," the guy to my left said. "Right, Calvin? Kill him?"

They weren't going to kill me.

You know that I live.

How would I write this otherwise?

"You guys fucking killed her," I said.

"We didn't," the guy on my right said.

"It's bad luck to kill an old lady," Calvin said. "We just scared her a little. Smashed the door in."

For some reason, I believed him. Violence can just show up, knock on your door.

CHAPTER ONE

I moved my arm up toward my shirt pocket, and one of the dudes flinched.

"I'm just reaching for my smokes," I said.

"No smoking," one of the guys said. "I'm allergic."

"He's a very sensitive dude," Calvin said.

"Where are we going anyway?" I asked.

"You know," Calvin said, "you used to be all right. I thought we could work with you, but this is a serious sign of disrespect."

"This?"

"Stealing our fucking dynamite!"

I couldn't deny it. I couldn't reason with him. I had pissed away all of my options, and then I had pissed on them again.

"Where is it?" he said. "If you give it back, we'll take it easy on you."

"It's gone," I said. "I blew up a dumpster out behind Burrito King. Melted the metal. People heard it for miles. You guys didn't hear that shit? It smelled like rotten burrito all night."

"When the fuck was this?"

"Two nights ago."

"You guys hear about this?" Calvin asked. He was peering over the backseat instead of looking out at the road.

"I didn't hear anything," one said.

The other shrugged. "He's full of shit."

"Fuck you," I said. Then I drove my elbow into the guy to my right, hard, and then into the guy to my left, even harder, smack in his jaw, and he spit up a tooth, and Calvin said, "Fucking hey," and he reached behind to grab me, and the car skipped up on the curb and smashed into a telephone pole. The hood crumpled, wrapped around that pole with a screech of bent-metal hug, and then the alarm whomped into full freakout mode.

"Fucking asshole," Calvin said.

He tried to bang the car into reverse, but we were stuck.

"Get out and push," he said. The alarm kept whomping.

The two guys jumped out, and I slid toward a door too, but it slammed in my face.

"Not you, motherfucker," Calvin said.

My heart was a single dried lentil. You need a big meaty heart to feel fear. I swung the door open and said, "I'll help or some shit," and then I just got out. The two dudes were in front of the car. Calvin was in the driver's seat.

"Stop him!" Calvin yelled, but by then I was out in the road. A red Mazda slowed down because otherwise it would have introduced parts of me to the tar and gravel, and all the while Calvin's car alarm swore at us.

Calvin couldn't even drive. There was no way he could have blown up a building. I thought that as I threw myself on the hood of the Mazda and stared through the windshield at a head of blondness. I flipped myself across to the passenger side, ripped open the door, and crawled onto some college girl's lap.

"Drive fast," I said. "Those dudes are trying to kill me."

For some reason, the blondness drove, perhaps in the fastest way she knew how, which was a calm, careful three miles over the speed limit, and she did not say "Oh, my gawd," even though you want her to.

The driver actually said, "How do you know we don't want to kill you too?"

And the girl who was my chair said, "Bethany!"

My chair smelled like shampoo, kumquats or some shit. Vitamin E. I am not objectifying her. She held me in her arms. She was a loving human and a chair. I honestly felt a kind of love, even though I didn't really see her face.

"I'll call the police," she said. "Let me get my phone."

"Don't," I said.

I kind of loved her. And Bethany too—she had a helium foot.

I thought they could take me home and soak my lentil heart, wherever their home was. They would make a soup of it. Instead I convinced them to drop me off downtown.

Calvin would be pissed, but that's been a given for hundreds of pages.

Those gals wouldn't even let me buy them a drink. That's the kind of gals they were. Their hair would never smell like hair. I think that counts as a minor tragedy, a trage-let.

All of this might seem like an aside, but my task is to serve you the truth, and that's what happened. And I should mention, too, that the fucking kid matters somehow. That poseur Dickensian urchin spawn of Calvin had some kind of bead on me. If I didn't already have a ghost, he could have applied for the position. He was qualified in every way except being dead.

He would come back. He will come back. You can turn to page 266 and find him, but that will be some other fresh, new sun-wiped day. You could flip forward, but I wouldn't fuck with time like that if I were you. Time's a dangerous thing. All day long we cut it up. All day long we snort it down.

CHAPTER ONE

When I was seven years old, I did have to beg sometimes. When I lived with my grandmother, who talked to angels and devils—she had time for both, a particular courtesy for devils—I often ate meals out of a garbage can.

It fortifies the stomach flora.

The microbe-laden pizza that would lay you out, that would turn your skin a vivid shade of puke, just infects me with nostalgia. I can eat seconds and have the rest for breakfast.

I don't think you should act like a beggar unless you are a beggar. My grandmother would say that to the angels. Sometimes she'd say it to them when I was standing right there. She stirred big pots of water on the stove and called it broth. She referred to the devils as *sir*. I wore the same pair of pants for a month.

She loved me in her own way.

She did not like to talk to humans. She had so many more interesting guests.

Can you see the family resemblance?

There's this part of me, some gland shaped like a bug, that thinks my grandmother had a Ghost Machine too. Maybe it was hooked up to a Victrola. Maybe her son came back to haunt her.

Don't worry me with questions of anatomy. I believe in all kinds of glands, all kinds of hormones. My brain is full of that shit. My whole life has been a quest for dopamine.

When you are thirteen and scared and polluted already, a pint of gin will smooth you out for a couple of hours. Wouldn't you pay twelve bucks for that?

~~Can you tell I was fucked from the beginning? That's how I~~ should have begun, really. Not *I am born*. *I am fucked*.

If I'm too honest for you, read some other fucking book.

CHAPTER ONE

I was born fucked.

And then things got even worse.

CHAPTER ONE

I wouldn't want my father to be my ghost. He convinced my mother to give up on life, to give up on me.

If they had taken me with them, I think I would be restless. I think I would have come back.

What if a baby haunted you? What would you do?

If you think a squalling baby is bad, wait until you see a ghost baby. It's coming. I see that ghost baby in your future.

Sometimes I feel like I don't even know my own self. Sometimes I say something, and then I think, *that's not me.* I used to think that after acts of violence: *That's not me. That's not me.*

But, of course, it was me.

CHAPTER ONE

I don't think you're getting it. I keep trying to explain, and you're all like, "Uh-huh, uh-huh," and then I see some sort of halo of uncertainty, up there circling your brain. Maybe it's not uncertainty. Maybe it's not a halo.

I think maybe you need to go back and reread. Please return to Chapter One and try this thing again.

CHAPTER ONE

Welcome back. I assure you you've missed nothing of value, either emotional or intellectual.

I think what happened, what just happened, is those two girls—benign Samaritans—unloosened something gooey in my brain. You would think I'd like the soft/firm one I sat on, but I actually liked the one who joked about wanting to kill me.

Maybe that wouldn't surprise you.

Maybe it wouldn't surprise you that they dropped me off downtown, not at the Replay but at the Taproom, which I considered a clever fucking venue-change curveball, and sitting at the bar, an unlit cigarette bobbing in her lips, was Saskia.

"Don't play it cool," she said.

"I won't," I said.

Her eyes were big, flat, wet at the corners.

She didn't look at me really, just pulled the unlit cigarette out of her mouth, wiggled the beer in her hand to watch the amber plane of the surface shift and shimmer.

"What happened with that girl you were with the other night?" she said.

"Uh, she thinks I killed Marilynne. I don't think we're simpatico anymore."

I watched her watching the beer that twitched and lurched in her hand.

"I would piss on your head," Saskia said, "but I would never accuse you of murder."

"Thanks," I said.

She nodded at the bartender. He poured whiskey into two shot glasses.

"To not playing it cool," I said.

We clinked glasses and drank it down.

I sat next to her and our shoulders brushed. I let them keep brushing.

She said, "You smell like a girl."

"I was just sitting on a girl!"

"I thought we weren't playing it cool."

"I'm being earnest," I said. "I'm trying it out, earnestness. I was literally sitting on a girl, who was sitting in a car that rescued me from Calvin."

We sat for a minute, then she said, "I appreciate your face, your earlobes. You have promising genitals. You are sometimes rather funny. Your dysfunction puts my life in clearer perspective."

"I think all that's ice-water territory," I said.

"It's not," she said. "Not at all."

She motioned to the bartender, and he refilled our glasses.

"To earnestness," she said.

"To not playing it cool," I said.

Our glasses tinked against one another.

"I was so worried you'd end up dead," she said. She was crying a little.

If she asked me to give things up, I would give it all up.

CHAPTER ONE

You wouldn't think it was that easy, but it was that easy.

It's not like I just happened to run into Saskia. It wasn't this great coincidence. I called her on my cell phone. I called her on the advice of those two gals who rescued me from Calvin.

"Call her," one said.

"*Call* her!" said the other.

Then, when I did, they fed me all my lines.

"Don't say you love her," one hissed at me.

"Say it!"

"Bethany, no!"

"I'm getting mixed signals on the love question," I said.

"What?" Saskia said.

"Tell her you're sorry," one said.

"I'm so fucking sorry," I said.

"I know," Saskia said. "You can be kind of a fucked-up dick."

"I love you," I said, and one of the gals gasped.

You didn't think I was capable of love, but I didn't think you were capable of reading a book.

CHAPTER ONE

"Also," she said, "you are not unattractive."

She said that at the Taproom, under the influence of whiskey and earnestness.

I can't remember the whole conversation because something fucked up happened or was about to happen. I'm sure you're surprised.

I am a great admirer of her caudal region. She has a sharp, feral face with a pointed chin, a pointed nose. She's all angles. A sloppy caricaturist would make her rodent-like. She has fierce niblet teeth, but as you know, I am anything but sloppy. She's not rodent-like. You're not looking closely enough. There's a feline touch to her eyes, their slightly wide set, and to the points of her ears. When she smiles, she's all human. She doesn't do it very often. She seldom blinks. She watches coolly.

She's both cat and mouse.

Her ribs show through her flesh. I've counted them with my tongue.

When I say her name, it's like pushing a raft into the water.

This doesn't make sense, yet I feel that it's true.

I've never been on a raft. I've peed in a river. I've been smacked in the head with an oar, but that was on dry land.

I have never pushed a raft into water, but I've said the name Saskia again and again. I've whispered it into her ear.

It's the same thing, basically. Embarkation. A beginning.

CHAPTER ONE

Saskia signaled to the bartender. I waited for the whiskey, but he walked into the back room.

Saskia and I talked, and we talked some more. She had a hand on my knee, and the day seemed like night, and the bar door opened and then shut behind us. I didn't even look, because if it was Calvin, I could deal with it—I could deal with anything—and then a cop put his hand on my shoulder.

He said my real name, and Saskia made a face.

"You're under arrest."

"Sorry," she said. "It's the only way."

Of course, you knew all along that the only place I could end up was jail. That was my destination. Maybe you think that's where I belong.

The cop scissored my arms behind my back and clipped them together with his handcuffs. Unless this has happened to you, you won't understand the full plight.

If you're handcuffed like this and start running and trip over something, you can't catch yourself. Your face will meet the pavement. If you need to scratch your nose, you're shit out of luck.

Saskia seemed to be crying.

"Don't call me a bitch," she said. "Don't even think it."

I was too forlorn to call her a bitch. I felt the whiskey in my veins.

"I know you didn't do it," she said. "This is the only way to get it over with."

The cop and his partner pushed me toward the door.

I looked back at Saskia. Her chin was this sharp delicate thing pointed at the floor. Everything she had pointed down. She was crying for real now, trembling.

The cops escorted me out the door.

The handcuffs didn't feel as cold as you'd think. It's almost as if they warmed them up for me.

That's when they read me my rights. I sat in the back of the squad car, and Marilynne's ghost sat next to me. It was nothing like the shit they do on TV. Your arms start to feel funny, go to pebbled sleep; your arms belong in front of you, or at your sides, but the police have a way of bending your contours.

Marilynne just sat there, with her dumb ghost face. I couldn't blink her away.

As you know, I have never exercised my right to remain silent.

I don't believe in silence, but I didn't call them motherfuckers until one of them said, "She's a good-looking chick, but she's a little freaky for my taste."

Both clauses of that sentence bothered me.

I motherfucked my right to silence away.

"We can add resisting arrest to the charges," one of the cops said. He was coming into focus: a young guy with sandy hair. He smiled a lot, no matter what he said.

"I'm resisting stupidity," I said, but I also stopped kicking at the window of the patrol car.

"Those things are impossible to kick out anyway," the other cop said. He's fuzzy in my memory. He was fuzzy back then. The other one had a big nose and that big fucking smile. His features were enough for two cops.

"What are you charging me with?" I asked.

"We've got enough to hold you on murder," Smiley said.

"You know she called, right, that she turned you in?" Fuzzy said.

"I know."

"Don't rub it in," Smiley said. "This fucker's on his way to jail."

They both sort of laughed in a rueful way.

CHAPTER ONE

The cops wanted to know about stuff. A tall lean guy with red hair and a beard asked most of the questions, frowned most of the frowns. He wrote notes in a notebook the size of a deck of cards.

They took my statement, and I told them just about everything I could remember, just about everything I told you.

"Did you touch anything?"

I had touched everything.

"Just her and the whiskey and the phone. And I almost slapped her head because of the fly. But I stopped myself. And the iron."

I tried to tell them the whole truth. I tried to tell them I didn't do it.

They asked me if her body still wore the oven mitt, and I couldn't remember. If I had already written this book, I could have pulled it out and turned to page 59 and checked, but this book didn't exist yet.

CHAPTER ONE

It's called Death by Hibachi. You can Google it.

It sounds like an all-you-can-eat special at a Japanese steak-house, but it's how my parents killed themselves.

I have this single black-and-white picture of them: This raff-ish partly Asian guy with black deadbolt eyes and a tall, slim tan woman who wanted to blend into the background. My father had on a black suit and a black shirt, no tie, and he held a bottle of Champagne. My mother held onto the wrist attached to the hand holding onto the bottle. She wore a white mini dress. They came out to Kansas to grow sunflowers; that's what I think anyway.

Who knows what went wrong. They did some petty crimes, and they were wanted for kiting checks. They didn't want a horrid, squawking baby. They didn't want to go to jail. They didn't want to sober up. They didn't want to grow sunflowers.

They bought eight charcoal grills and set them up in the living room of their rented house, sealed up the doors and the windows with old T-shirts, newspaper, and duct tape, squirted lighter fluid, flicked matches. Then they breathed in the sweet, sleepy smoke of carbon monoxide until they couldn't breathe anymore.

Maybe they saw visions, or maybe they just saw the world as it really is. I'm not sure which is worse.

I was two days old. They left me outside on the front lawn in a cheap plastic bassinet. They left me on purpose, I guess. I guess they did me some sort of favor. All I could do was stare straight up and scream. The sky must have been an Easter-egg pastel, a blue you need to search for.

Sometimes I imagine that I'm still that lost shithead baby, looking up at that sky, and sometimes I'm the one who finds the baby, and I pick him up, and I mumble bullshit gibberish at him, and I lie and say everything will be okay.

CHAPTER ONE

For all of my life, I've felt the need to keep moving.

Sometimes I remember something that I should have told you earlier.

Sometimes I write that thing down.

A neighbor found me actually. That's what I heard, anyway.

Pretend we just went through the long, boring part where I got all sensitive. Let's pretend there was fifty pages of that.

CHAPTER ONE

I believe in the power of defunct technology.

All books are about the pleasure of pages accumulating in your left hand, the glee of them disappearing from your right. Ruffle them a little. Go ahead. It's okay.

Don't you love the accumulation of pages in your left hand? We're moving now!

CHAPTER ONE

If you're reading this on an electronic device, then fuck you.

CHAPTER ONE

The Douglas County Jail lurks outside of town, by the corn-fields and the rental storage units made out of corrugated steel. All the crap people don't want but just can't get rid of is sent out there: boxes of 45s, spare auto parts, dead grandma's sofa, assorted criminal types such as myself.

I was handed a banana-yellow jumpsuit. They took all my stuff. The underwear they supply is made out of Kleenex, and I ripped mine nearly in half, but they wouldn't give me another pair. They stripped me down and yelled at me.

The cops took pictures of my face from different angles. I held up one of those little signs with the numbers. It makes you feel the way you'd think—not very good, that's all I'm saying.

I was used to all the attention, though. I had done my time in juvie, down in Wichita. There's a rhythm to those places. You just need to follow the beat. A fat guard with a buzz cut walked me through the electric doors and then up an elevator, then through more doors until we got to a gray cinder room with a gray cinder cot and a hole in the floor to shit in and a gray cinder blanket and no pillow. I actually felt comfortable there. It was like coming home. Sure, your mother was pissed at you, and your brother wanted to beat the crap out of you when the lights went out, and your uncle was a pervert, but isn't that home?

I had lived in worse places.

"It's a good place to sober up," the guard said.

"I am sober," I said.

The Marilynne ghost stood in my cell. For the first time, I almost liked having her there. If she could watch over me, I felt like I could watch over her. We didn't need words.

They hadn't even let me make a phone call. I couldn't remember if that one-phone-call thing was real or something made up for TV.

CHAPTER ONE

They put me in the Special Management pod, which is another concept that might sound pretty good in a different context.

I'd get to stay in my cell for twenty-three hours out of every twenty-four.

As long as you pretend you're not alive, jail can be fine. Jail time is an empty bucket that you have to fill up.

All you can do is piss in it.

I could only think of one person who would absolutely definitely come and bail me out, but Marilynne had been dead for almost two hundred pages.

CHAPTER ONE

The scream thrashed through my ears, and I woke into that moment, woke into that sound. I tried to take it in: the yelling voice, the strange stiff cot under me, the darkness, the death of Marilynne sitting in my brain, the ghost of Marilynne in the corner, the rough snaky itch on my wrist where a handcuff had bit away at me.

He screamed again: "I didn't do anything."

I had thought it was a fake voice, but it was real.

It was the dog-man who had called me with Marilynne's cell phone, who said, "Don't go home."

In the cell next to mine, he was coming down from something, and he was coming down hard, like an egg thrown off a roof. The yolk of this guy must have been splattered on a street somewhere. He kept yelling and yelling.

"I didn't do anything! I didn't do anything!"

Then I could hear the background fuzz of the jail speaker. The guard was talking to him over the PA.

"Just settle down," the guard said. "Settle down."

Then louder: "Settle down, settle the fuck down."

"I didn't do anything."

"Settle down."

They played out that call and response for I don't know how long, and I lay there in the soupy blackness of night, listening.

CHAPTER ONE

When they let us out for that hour, if I had the chance, I could bludgeon him with my lunch tray. It was the only weapon I could find. We didn't even have shoelaces.

When I was thirteen, I almost choked a guy to death, but he made it through and found the Lord, and I spent those six months at a juvenile detention center. That's all supposed to be sealed up and forgotten now, but I want credit for turning that guy on to God. I didn't even know his name. It was one of those things. It could happen to anybody. Maybe not you, but almost anybody.

You might wonder if I could still do something like that, and I could, but most of the time, I don't think I would.

This will have to suffice for human development.

CHAPTER ONE

About twelve of us were banana-suited guests of Douglas County, but I didn't care about anyone except him.

I sat across from him at a table bolted to the floor. The chairs were bolted too.

He was several degrees more fucked up than I was.

He looked like he had been wrung out and hung up on a clothesline. He had a sheen of sweat on him, and his left hand was shaking. His right didn't quiver at all.

"Ain't that fucked up," he said. He held out his left hand, then his right.

Left: "Shaky," he said.

Right: "Ain't shaky," he said. "It almost makes me want to shake it on purpose."

I just looked at him. His voice was real. He really talked like that, barked like that.

His face was thin. His bones looked sharp under the skin. He had pale blue eyes, an expiring blue, like the sheen of skim milk. Those eyes didn't seem to belong in such a face, in such a setting.

"What did you do?" he said to me.

"Nothing," I said. I picked at my left thumbnail with my right index finger, spunked out some grit.

"Hah," he said, "me too. But what did you really do?"

"Nothing. What about you?"

"Nothing," he said.

The dirt was stuck under my other fingernail now. I imagined passing it back and forth under my fingernails forever. I looked at my hands, but I could tell he was looking at me. His look had a weight to it, and I turned and cocked my head up toward him.

He watched me, and I watched him back. I felt a hot burr of words stuck somewhere. He didn't flinch. We sat there looking into each other's noses, eyes, hairs, veins, arteries, capillaries, pores. He had a couple of blackheads. He had short blond hair. He had a black tattoo, just a squiggly line, growing out of his yellow jumpsuit, writhing up his neck.

"Look at us," he said, "just a couple of assholes."

"Yeah," I said. "What's your name?"

"Howard," he said. "Howard Asshole."

"My name's Neptune," I said.

His face quirked, but he caught himself.

"That's a made-up name," he said.

"I'm Neptune," I said, and I tried to look at him in a cellular way. He still didn't flinch.

"Neptune Asshole," he said, "like we're brothers."

I met Howard Donaldson at the Douglas County Jail. The police arrested him approximately six hours after they busted me. He was fucked up on meth, had been for days. He blew through a red light in a stolen car and got pulled over. He had all kinds of outstanding warrants. His luck was as bad as mine, worse even.

He had the cell next door to me. We could whisper to each other through the walls.

CHAPTER ONE

A raccoon hunched up its back and looked at me. We had a moment of mammalian recognition, and as I looked into its black eyes, like lumps of charcoal that were burning down to hot dust, I knew it was dead. It was a ghost of a raccoon. I felt the sweaty idea of this wrap around my neck, and the raccoon sort of nodded, then scuttled away. It was dead and gone, and I wondered how many ghosts were out there, pigeon ghosts on the roof and cat ghosts dreaming about those pigeons.

In my cell, ghosts accumulated and then dispersed.

A ghost snake slithered in and out of my vision, and I had to dig a long time before the memory came loose: I had killed it, for no reason at all, with a heavy rock when I was six or seven. A dog I didn't know gloomed in. A ghost dog never feels at home, never sits, never belongs to anyone anymore.

Thousands of ghost bugs flittered, buzzed soundlessly. Or maybe it was the same five bugs again and again, seeping into the room, then out.

The ghosts made no sound. That seems like the greatest drawback of death: the unceasing silence. *Okay*, the world says, *now we mean it: you'll never be heard again.*

If they all accumulated at once, the cell couldn't hold them.

Only Marilynne stayed the whole time.

Marilynne and I watched the ghost birds, the ghost worms, the fossil ghosts, the ghost squirrels, the ghost beetles, the ghost flies that almost seemed alive.

CHAPTER ONE

When it's all over, where will you end up?

CHAPTER ONE

Ghosts have a calming presence once you get used to them.

They're a form of downer.

You could OD on that shit.

A ghost fly hovered in the air, but it was buzzless. It wasn't a real fly, or at least it wasn't a live one. I tried to figure out if it smelled like gin.

For a while, I thought all of those ghosts were things I somehow killed.

How many bugs have you killed?

But then I thought, did I ever kill a raccoon? A Scottie dog with a wool sweater?

And I didn't kill Marilynne. I've never killed anything bigger than a snake.

I think the ghosts just liked me for some reason.

Maybe they were speaking to me in some ghost language and I just wasn't dead enough to hear.

I don't think ghosts have emotions or intellects. I think ghosts are all instinct.

If you're ghost bait, they're drawn to you.

I don't think it's even about the ghosts. I think the problem is being the fucking bait.

CHAPTER ONE

I began to tell Howard Donaldson about my ghosts.

"I can see all these ghost bugs I crushed with the palm of my hand," I said. "Beetles I crunched, roaches, sure, too many roaches."

"You're fucked up, man," he said, and he wasn't quite whispering.

"That old lady's ghost is here," I said. "I can see it. Her face is mashed in with an iron."

"You're full of shit, dude."

"Her name was Marilynne," I said, "and you called me after you did it. You said, 'Don't go home.'"

He didn't say anything.

"She's here, man," I said. "You did it. You know you did it."

"Fuck you," he said.

"She's just standing here, face stove in, lip cracked, eye busted open."

The intercom crackled, meaning a guard was about to announce something.

"Everything all right in there?" a guard asked.

"Fuck, man," Howard Asshole said. "I've got to talk to the fucking sheriff."

"No profanity allowed," the guard said.

"I mean it," Howard Asshole said. "I've got to talk to the sheriff."

"What do you need?" the guard said. It was more of a command than a question.

"To confess. I killed somebody."

We heard grumbling over the PA.

"It's the worst thing I've done," Howard Asshole said, and then he said, quieter, "Is she really there?"

"Yeah," I said.

"It seems like she's haunting the wrong one."

"I've done some awful things too," I said. "I used to keep doing them."

We could hear the guards being buzzed into the pod.

"Where's the murderer?" one of them asked.

"Over here," Howard Asshole said.

They buzzed him out of his cell and handcuffed him. They weren't gentle about it.

"See you, Neptune Asshole," he said.

"Shut up," one of the guards said.

CHAPTER ONE

None of this seemed to bring the Marilynne ghost any pleasure. When you're dead, you're dead.

She stood there in my cell, this sentry, as I did push-ups, as I read *Huck Finn*, as I ate my plain white bread smeared with peanut butter, no jelly.

We waited for Howard Asshole to come back, but he didn't come back.

That's about all I know about him: he warned me not to go home, he declared me his brother, he confessed to murder.

Apparently Howard Asshole was fucked up on meth, drunk, forlorn, and he stumbled on an opportunity. A door was smashed open. He thought he'd clean out whatever the burglars didn't take. He'd just scavenge, vulturize, which is not a word, but it's how he thought of it. I'm recreating this here. This is what I heard.

Except he didn't find an empty burgled house. He found Marilynne.

The house was a mess. A spray-painted message was on the wall. He thought it was my house, Neptune's house.

Marilynne somehow got her cell phone, and she called me—the least likely savior—and Howard Asshole tried to smash the phone out of her hand with the nearest thing he could grab, an iron primed for cotton. It hissed out steam as he slammed it into her.

Do you see how I give him the benefit of the doubt? Maybe he wasn't trying to kill her.

Even he, even Howard Asshole, tried to respect life in some way. He failed at it, but he tried. I think he tried.

She's dead anyway. Even her ghost is gone now.

CHAPTER ONE

The other ghosts disappeared. It was just me and Marilynne.

Howard Asshole wouldn't have wandered in there if I hadn't taken the dynamite and pissed off the anarchists. They wouldn't have smashed down her door.

I blamed myself for all of this, and then I did it again.

Still do.

I apologized to her ghost, and then I did it again.

I meant it fully and completely this time.

She stood right before me, closer than she'd ever been.

The bad eye cleared up, the wound disappeared, and then something about her face looked shinier, tighter, and then she had a thinner face, and then her hair grew suddenly longer, and then it became shorter. Her eyes no longer protruded. Her double chin disappeared. Her wrinkles smoothed out, except for the crinkles around her mouth.

I couldn't stop shivering, and I just kept getting older. Every second seemed to count, and Marilynne just looked at me with those dumb eyes. I wasn't cold, but my skin was wiggling, and my insides were wiggling, and my bones were still, and my hair was alive and electric.

She became thinner. The dress shrunk with her.

Parts of her curved in; parts curved out.

Her lips looked bigger, her eyes larger.

The crinkles around her mouth evened out. A dimple formed in her chin.

Her hair grew down her back, longer and longer, then it snapped up to her shoulders.

She grew smaller.

Her teeth bucked out. Her eyes got smaller.

Her curves disappeared.

She lost several inches and then several more.

Her ears shrunk.

She came up to my hip.

She came up to my knee.

She was on the floor, trying to crawl.

She rolled on her back.

She was a baby, raising her little fists.

She squirmed.

She went still.

She was gone.

I watched the empty place where she lay for a long, long time.

CHAPTER ONE

At first, I thought she was degrading, wearing away, but I was as wrong about that as I am about many, many things. She was headed back to zero, to the beginning, to when we are pure.

The whole devolution took thirty seconds, maybe less. I didn't clock it or anything.

For half a beat, she was this fucked-up kind of beautiful, this gorgeous fuck-up—I could tell she was a fuck-up even then—and her hair ran all the way down her back, and something pinged inside of me, and I thought, *what if I knew her then?*

Mainly, though, I felt light-socket jabbed, fried and tingled. The current of her backward life ran through me. It made a circuit of my brain.

I don't know what the hell happened to her. I bet you don't either.

Not even Saskia could figure this shit out, and she's so much smarter than both of us put together.

CHAPTER ONE

I'll never know what I really meant to Marilynne. I'll never get to make amends.

It isn't fair, but here's how I used to picture her: scared of her students, and scared of her fingernails, and scared of "little people," and scared of the hallway, and scared of the rug in the hallway, and scared of the floor beneath the rug. Scared of pretzels. Scared of the noise outside right now. It could be someone screaming, or it could be bad brakes. Scared of dirt, which leads her back to her fingernails, which are even scarier now. They look kind of greenish under certain lights.

Marilynne was gone, and so were her big flabby mouth and her British-lady hats that looked as if they had swooped down and perched on her head. She was approximately four foot eleven. Her face was round, ovaled with wine fat, and her eyes had a fuzzy gray-blue clarity.

Marilynne with her puffed-rice face and her hat that looked like a work boot. Marilynne with her sad cumulonimbus eyes.

I'm not being fair. I'm never fair to her. I'm never fair to anyone.

Except you, I'm fair to you.

CHAPTER ONE

They made me stew for long time. Maybe it wasn't stewing. Maybe it was some kind of braise, a marinade.

I can't give blood because I was in jail for more than seventy-two hours. I didn't even get buggered. I didn't even bugger anyone.

Sure, my mind got fucked, but that happens all the time.

I finished *Huck Finn*, and then I started *Copperfield*. They had both books down in the jail library.

Tax was in that jail somewhere, and then Calvin and a bunch of anarchists showed up too. An anonymous tip led to a raid at the anarchists' house.

Okay, the tip wasn't anonymous. I turned snitch.

Isn't that the gateway to writing memoir?

I knew they had weapons, sawed-off shotguns and shit like that.

If I hadn't run off with his dynamite, Calvin would have probably faced twice as many years. That's what I do for people: I take the years right off. They melt away.

They let me out before I had to start reading *Moby Dick*. I think that whale was an orphan too.

They had a confession for Marilynne's murder—Howard Asshole's story checked out. They couldn't hold me for all of the minor sins I'd committed. They could guess at them, but they couldn't charge me.

If they could, think about how much time you'd serve for all the little things you do, for lying and for going five miles over the speed limit and for thinking cruel and pointless thoughts about the people who love you.

"Do I get an apology?" I asked the guard who processed me before my release back into civilization.

He looked at me, then tucked the side of his mouth into half a sneer.

"You get no such thing," he said. "Now get the fuck out of here."

He gave me back my stuff: my phone, my wallet, my shoelaces.

"I'm going to sue," I said, because it seemed like the thing to say.

"You ain't suing nothing," the guard said, "and you know it."

CHAPTER ONE

The only good part about jail is they take away your phone.

CHAPTER ONE

Marilynne was killed by a guy looking for money and drugs. It was this kid named Howard Donaldson, and he lived in Kansas City. He was churning on crank and his car found Marilynne's driveway.

I didn't know him at all. Marilynne didn't know him. You think maybe I'm a dirtbag, but a guy like that might be driving by your house right now. You're better off hanging out with me. Don't look out the window. Don't spark his attention. If he's out there, let him drive past. Stay here with me. I have something to tell you.

There weren't any clues.

The only true mystery is the way life dispenses luck.

That's the greatest mystery of all.

I told you you weren't going to solve anything.

CHAPTER ONE

I got Jimmyhead to help me clear out my trashed apartment. We threw everything in the back of his pickup truck. We went up and down the stairs with armloads of crushed books. We slid the ripped mattress down the stairs. We threw handfuls of old clothes.

We each grabbed an end of the couch and started the awkward trek down the stairs.

"Are you okay?" he said as he backed down. "You got it?"

"I'm okay."

"Are you sure?"

"I'm sure."

"Are you sure you're sure?"

That's when my phone dinged, and I sort of let go of my end of the couch. The force of it pushed Jimmyhead down the stairs, and then he went under. The couch clattered and shifted and banged right over him.

Jimmyhead looked kind of oily and withered.

"I think I'm concussed," he said, "and I think the couch popped my left testicle."

I shrugged.

"Why do you have to be such an asshole?"

I didn't think I was being an asshole, but I'd been wrong about these things before.

"It was my phone," I said, and I pulled it out. I had a text message from my service provider. They wanted me to pay my bill and the one before that and the one before that.

"You owe me beer," Jimmyhead said.

"I owe you beer."

"You owe me whiskey."

"I owe you whiskey."

"Now!"

I left him lying on the stairs. I walked the eight blocks to the liquor store.

When I got back, Jimmyhead looked slightly stoned. His eyes were more pink than white, and his hair seemed a bit chuffed about being styled by a couch. It blossomed everywhere like little tufts of brown grass.

"Dude?" I said.

"Dude," he replied solemnly.

"You okay?"

He didn't answer, just held out his hand for one of my beers.

"Drink it fast," I said, "and it won't hurt as much."

We gulped.

"I've decided to kinda go to law school," he said.

"Oh, man."

"Dude," he said in his solemn way.

"Is this about Marilynne?" I said. "Has she made you rethink your life path?"

"All of life isn't about fucking Marilynne."

"What's this all about, then?"

"Marilynne," he said.

"Would Marilynne really want you to act like such a depressed shithead?" I asked.

"Probably," he said.

He stuck out his hand for another beer.

"They grow on you," he said.

"It's an acquired taste really," I said.

We drank, and it tasted like fungus, like something growing in your esophagus.

"Here's to law school," I said, and I twisted off the whiskey cap, swigged from the bottle. It tasted like the burn of a match. I handed him the bottle.

"A girl came by to see you while you were gone. Just looking at her sort of reinflated my testicle."

"What girl?"

He took a gulp of whiskey. "You are conditionally forgiven," he said. "I tried to give the girl the couch, but she didn't want it."

"Bad things have happened on that couch."

"Bad things happen on every couch."

"They flatten our asses," I said.

"American couches—the silent killer."

"Who was it?"

"Just a girl," he said.

"Saskia?"

"Never seen her before. But she smelled nice. She resurrected me with her smells."

"Did she have wide-set eyes, like real blue?"

"I don't know," he said. "She was good-looking, man, and she smelled nice, like pistachio ice cream and oranges."

"Did you tell her I was coming back?"

"I told her you were done, that you're leaving town, that you're practically gone."

"Why didn't you tell her to wait?"

"You said, and I quote, 'Fuck this place and everyone in it.'"

His quotation was accurate.

I pshhed open a can of beer and then another. We drank for a while.

"You going to miss this place?" he asked.

I shook my head, my mouthful of beer.

CHAPTER ONE

I put three shirts and two pairs of pants and some socks and some underwear in my backpack, and then I stuffed in just one book and then another.

"Man," Jimmyhead said, "this is your life."

All my other stuff was just loose in the back of the pickup. It rattled and sloshed around.

We drove down the alley between Massachusetts and New Hampshire and threw my life into the dumpster behind the Bottleneck.

We pitched in the couch and the trashed paperbacks and my clothes and, finally, my cell phone.

"You keeping that backpack?" he asked. He eyed it like he wanted me to throw it in too.

"Dude," I said. "I'm pitching out the rest of my life."

"I'm just askin.'"

We looked at the dumpster crammed with all my stuff.

From deep within it, I could hear my phone chiming away.

CHAPTER ONE

I went to the cash machine, and three times I attempted to withdraw exactly $27.12 from my account, its entire contents. Three times the machine impolitely rejected this request.

Finally, I settled on a desire for twenty-five dollars, and the machine spit out my money and a receipt. My $2.12 was spinning around within the circuits of that ATM. What did the machine need my 212 cents for?

I was on my way back to the Replay with my crisp bills, a five and a twenty; they smelled saladly, and I rubbed them together as if friction would create more of them in some economic-slash-sexual way.

The guy who always plays the saxophone downtown was playing his saxophone downtown.

Outside the Red Lyon, Calvin's beggar child wheedled five of my bucks off me.

"He's not even my real dad," he said.

We tried to wink at each other, but his heart wasn't in it. He didn't even bob his head.

He nearly bankrupted me.

Lawrence's big freckled face kissed me on the cheek and whispered in my ear. It would all be okayish; I would survive; I would drink a beer and tip my server with generosity and perhaps wit; I would use semicolons correctly.

CHAPTER ONE

I would have one last drink, and then I'd hit the road.

Except my math was off. I drank for a long while.

Random people bought me shots.

Right after last call, I slipped through the crowd. A girl I once slept with didn't say a word but patted me on the cheek. A guy named Lunchmeat high-fived me.

I circled the patio.

I headed down Massachusetts for the last drunken time.

I thought about sleeping under a tree. When the world resurrected itself, I would be ready. I would already be out there. I would be breathing the morning air before anyone else. I would leave town before the day began.

These thoughts pelted me like hail, little icy cubes that beat away at me.

Then I heard the sound of running footsteps.

I waited for a person. You hear footsteps, you expect a person. It seemed reasonable. I felt the cold plink of a thought: this could be fucking anyone. Maybe someone would shiv me before I left town.

I could see the person. It was small, thin. I thought maybe it was made out of pretzels, those hard little sticks that crush each other in a Ziploc bag.

I made my fist into a harder fist, tight knuckleboned possibility, and it made the muscles tug up in my forearm.

As the pretzel man ran toward me, it became a pretzel woman, and then it became Saskia, and she yelled, "Boo," and my fingers collapsed back into being a hand.

She panted and she panted some more, and I grabbed her chin in my hand and turned it and licked her cheek.

"Salty," I said.

She snapped her head away and shook off my hand. "You are so fucked up," she said.

"I want you near."

"What?"

"Nothing," I said.

"I'm always saying what, and you're always saying nothing."

"That's not true. Sometimes we switch."

I tried to reach out for her chin again, and she snapped it back.

"You ran all this way so I wouldn't touch you?"

"Come here then," she said, and I stepped toward her.

"I'm not going to hurt you," Saskia said.

"Oh," I said.

"Don't sound so disappointed."

She held my face by the sides, and she leaned in, and she angled my head down until our foreheads touched. I stared into her big old eyes.

"I'm sorry," she said. "It seemed like the only way. Do you believe me?"

"I don't not believe you."

"It's a start," she said.

Saskia slipped her arms around my neck, and I slipped mine around her waist. Our lips pressed together. With my left hand, I felt her right hip, the perfect curve of a perfect arc of a Frisbee.

We pushed our foreheads together so our eyes fused and became anime, larger than life. Her soul wasn't in there, but I saw flecks of ground-up glass, bits of her brain, the pulse of blue neon, the stars after difficulties.

CHAPTER ONE

When I went to the dumpster to get my stuff back the next day, a freegan hippie kid was already pulling things out of the trash.

"All this shit's mine," I said.

"Garbage is for the people," he said. He had long, blond, stringy hair and a red Miami Heat headband. I couldn't remember his name.

"We could share it," I said. "I'm people too."

"Are these your shirts?" he asked. "How come you didn't throw out any clean ones?" He sniffed one right in the armpit.

"You can wash them."

"Maybe."

We dug out the couch, some jeans, the ripped mattress.

I unearthed some of my books.

"You ever read Kafka?" I asked him.

"Dude turns into a bug?" he said. "Skimmed it."

"Skimmed it?"

"Cliffs Notes."

We worked some more. The dumpster smelled like rancid beer.

"I'd like to read a book," he said, "about a bug who turns into a man."

He found the phone, which he held up and into the sunlight, arm fully stretched, as if it were a torch or a magical sword, but I guess he was just checking for reception.

"Still charged," he said. "You wanna call anyone?"

"Nope," I said. "You can have it."

"Fucking thing's obsolete."

He threw it back in.

CHAPTER ONE

Each time I start again, it gives me the illusion of control.
Each time you turn the page, I bet it gives you that illusion too.

CHAPTER ONE

I almost called this "I Am Not Calling This Chapter One."

I don't like how that whole fucking conceit gives you an excuse, a reason—maybe it's a pathology—to never actually follow through with anything.

I could tell you were writing about me sometimes by the look on your face.

It didn't happen like that. I did squat over you, sure, okay. But it seemed like a dirty and necessary kindness.

Actually it did happen that way. But I don't know why you had to write about it.

I can vouch, though, that you are telling some form of the truth. Whatever that's worth.

I didn't like the part when you fucked what'sherface or when you wanted to fuck the ghost. I think you wanted to fuck her anyway. And about the unprotected sex with what'sherface—thanks for telling me, asshole.

Also, that cave was disgusting.

And I did lie to you three times, but we've said a million things to each other, so my percentage of truth is pretty damn high. It's statistically significant that I almost always tell you the truth. That sliver of falsehood barely exists.

Are these sentences supposed to add up to a chapter?

I don't think yours do either.

I guess I think most of what you wrote is pretty fair, somewhat accurate.

But there's nothing rodenty about me. Feline, fine; I appreciate that. I took some other notes. I have talking points, concerns, worries, emendations, corrections, and real and substantial suggestions for style and clarity. And actual grammar tips.

All of this, and I still think I love you, and I only think you're a little bit of an asshole, a part-time one, like most of us.

Forget the rest of this actually, but please reconsider rodent-like.

And why didn't you tell me about your parents?

CHAPTER ONE

That last chapter was guest-written by Saskia, who said she wouldn't read this until I was done and happy, but I don't think you can be done and happy with anything.

Saskia and I have been hanging out. By that I mean that we sleep in the same bed every night, but it is far easier to call it hanging out.

She just asked me if she could go back and revise what she wrote in the last chapter, and I just told her, "No, never, impossible," and she gave me a fake-sad frown that made me want to suck up her bottom lip. It would become one of the pink curling folds of my brain.

"I just wrote that we're hanging out," I say.

"Is that what we're doing?" she says.

"I'm finishing a book," I say.

She waves her hand in a way that makes me think of the act of relinquishing.

It's not necessarily a bad thing. If it wasn't for all of the shit before, maybe we wouldn't have ended up in this kind of now.

We've caught up to the present. I sometimes thought we'd never make it.

When I stand up at meetings and say, "My name's Neptune, and I'm an alcoholic," everyone says back, "Hello, Neptune."

You've probably seen it on TV.

Saskia and I both go.

I still do stupid stuff, but it's somewhat less stupid than it used to be. That comma scab isn't even a scab anymore.

CHAPTER ONE

I couldn't help but think it was all connected. I tried to draw a chart that zipped from me to Marilynne to Saskia to Allen to Howard Asshole to Tax to my parents to Marilynne again to Casey to Jimmyhead to the cops to Calvin. I looked for patterns. I had all of these people on the perimeter of a circle, and then I drew lines between all of these people, and then I had a circle practically filled in with black. It kind of looked like this:

●

Something about it nearly stopped me.

CHAPTER ONE

I believe in a higher power, if we can somehow consider this book a higher power.

It's a piece of shit, of course, but it's worth thinking about.

CHAPTER ONE

In the end, maybe all books are about loneliness.

But not yet. I don't have to surrender to it yet. I can turn back to page 30, when she was still alive, when I could hear her voice.

And you're still here with me, right?

I'm still here with you.

I haven't finished yet.

If you think this book sucks, remember that you only read Chapter One. It could get better. There's always that possibility.

ACKNOWLEDGMENTS

There are too many people to thank and not enough pages to list them all and not enough brain cells to remember, but here goes.

Thank you to Iain Ellis (who is not in any way Uncle X), Mark Scoggins (who is not in any way Jimmyhead), Richard Noggle (who was Noggin but got cut out of the book), Kirby Fields, Emily Stamey, Shawn Thomson, Mike Stigman, Kate Lorenz, Mary Wharff, Katie Conrad, Cliff Phillips, Adam Powell, Emily Wicktor, Greg Brister, Andrea Weis, the Replay Lounge, Carolyn Jewers, Megan Kaminski, Justin Runge, Harbour Lights, the Taproom, the Dusty, the Pig, the Raven, La Prima Tazza, the Paradise Diner (RIP), La Guerre, the Self Graduate Fellowship, all the Hansons and Ballards and Hanson-Ballards, including Bear and Kingsley, and all the other people and entities that make me miss and love Lawrence, Kansas, every day, sometimes twice a day. (Please note: these parentheticals are legally binding!) Carolyn Doty was a pint-sized force of fiction. Tom Lorenz is a true friend and mentor.

Thank you to everyone at Dzanc Books: Michelle Dotter, Guy Intoci, Michael J. Seidlinger. Dan Wickett, and Steven Gillis. Steven Seighman, this cover is so fucking great. Thank you,

Kim Church, Carmiel Banasky, and Andrew F. Sullivan. To all of the anonymous copy editors out there, I will learn your names, sing them too.

At Kansas State University, thank you, Elizabeth Dodd, Karin Westman, Phil Nel, Anne Phillips, Traci Brimhall, Cameron Leader-Picone, Chris Nelson, and Jerry Dees. At Baldwin-Wallace University, thank you, Ted Harakas, Margaret Stiner (you too, Mike Riley), Sharon Kubasak, and Frank Paino. Most of all, thank you to my students, who challenge me and make me laugh and allow me to think about cool shit and once in a while infuriate me but almost never bore me.

In Manhattan, Kansas, thank you, Arrow Coffee and Bluestem and, fuck, fine, Radina's too, and thanks to Headlight Rivals, the Church of Swole, Field Day Jitters (RIP), Auntie Mae's, and this town's branch of the Dusty Bookshelf (may you rise again).

Christopher Rhodes, thanks for believing. Thanks to all the people who have ever pulled me out of the slush pile: I was drowning in there. Thank you, Trudy Lewis and Jack Vernon. Thank you, Rick Harsch. Thank you, John Wei. Thank you, Philip Rogers. Thank you, Noy Holland. Thank you, Craig Finn and the Hold Steady. Thank you, Paul D. and Frances Gumm. Thank you to all of my students back in the day at the Douglas County Jail.

Thank you, Shirley Kinnie Hoyt, and Karen and Rob Frankel, and Ross and Aaron Frankel and the McGreers and the Shewmakers and the Petersons.

Thanks again, coffee, and thank you, club soda, and you too, generic Paxil. Thank you to Frightened Rabbit, DTCV, the serendipitous Neptune sign along the bike path in the Cleveland Metroparks, every band I've ever seen that didn't suck, Steve Earle, Mates of State and Denis Johnson, Sleater-Kinney and gluten-free cupcakes, the Rural Alberta Advantage and Rainer Maria (not the poet). Thanks to literary magazines and the people who make them.

Thanks, Sarah and Seyvion and Sareya and Su'von—for being everything.

This book lived for way more than a decade and in four different houses before it came into your hands. On July 4, 2014, Sarah McGreer Hoyt started reading the first complete draft, came out to the porch at 1819 Poyntz Avenue in Manhattan, Kansas, where I was mowing the front lawn, and yelled, "Jesus Christ, kill your fucking darlings!"

Sorry, love. It's all darlings.